Jessica Steele is a star of Harlequin Romance®
and the author of more than 75 books.

Praise for

JESSICA STEELE:

About THE TROUBLE WITH TRENT

"Jessica Steele delights readers with top-notch
characterization, vivid scenes and a fresh twist...."
—*Romantic Times*

About THE SISTER SECRET

"Ms. Steele pens a touching love story...."
—*Romantic Times*

Jessica Steele is loved by readers around the world
for her entertaining, emotional and sparkling stories.

Jessica Steele lives in a friendly English village with her super husband, Peter. They are owned by a gorgeous Staffordshire bull terrier called Florence, who is boisterous and manic, but also adorable. It was Peter who first prompted Jessica to try writing and, after the first rejection, encouraged her to keep on trying. Luckily, with the exception of Uruguay, she has so far managed to research inside all the countries in which she has set her books, traveling to places as far apart as Siberia and Egypt. Her thanks go to Peter for his help and encouragement.

Books by Jessica Steele

HARLEQUIN ROMANCE®
3680—PART-TIME MARRIAGE
3695—HIS PRETEND MISTRESS
3721—A PROFESSIONAL MARRIAGE

AN ACCIDENTAL ENGAGEMENT
Jessica Steele

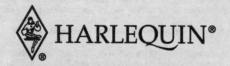

HARLEQUIN®

TORONTO • NEW YORK • LONDON
AMSTERDAM • PARIS • SYDNEY • HAMBURG
STOCKHOLM • ATHENS • TOKYO • MILAN • MADRID
PRAGUE • WARSAW • BUDAPEST • AUCKLAND

ISBN 0-373-03741-4

AN ACCIDENTAL ENGAGEMENT

First North American Publication 2003.

This edition published by arrangement with Harlequin Books S.A.

® and TM are trademarks of the publisher. Trademarks indicated with ® are registered in the United States Patent and Trademark Office, the Canadian Trade Marks Office and in other countries.

Visit us at www.eHarlequin.com

Printed in U.S.A.

CHAPTER ONE

SHE stirred in her sleep. She felt troubled, and her eyelids fluttered. She tried to recall what she was troubled about, but could not remember. She opened her eyes and lay there quietly, for a moment or two at relative peace with her world.

That peace was not to last. Suddenly her eyes widened— not only could she not remember what it was that troubled her, she could not remember anything! Could not remember anything at all. Everything was a complete blank!

Striving hard to keep a lid on her feeling of panic, she fought to remember something, even the tiniest detail, but there was nothing there. She could not even remember her own name!

She looked around her, but the pink walls of the room were alien to her; she did not recognise them. Involuntarily she cried out and tried to sit up—and discovered she barely had the strength to raise her head from her pillow.

But she was not alone. Alerted by her cry, a plump woman in a nurse's uniform came swiftly over to her bed. 'You're back with us, I see,' she said softly, calmly.

The young woman in the bed did not feel calm. 'Who are…? Where am…? I don't know where I am, who I am,' she whispered, her voice a panicking thread of sound.

The nurse was efficient and in no time a doctor was there in the room with them. After that, time passed for the young woman in a confusing semi-vacuum of visitors in white coats, of questions and tests, of medication and sedatives and a twilight world of drifting in and out of sleep.

Nurses attended to her healing cuts and bruises, but she

made no progress in remembering who she was. She had lost her memory.

On different occasions she surfaced to find one or other of two expensively suited males in her room. They made frequent calls to her bedside. One was tall and comfortably built. He was somewhere in his mid-forties, and she seemed to vaguely realise that he was a consultant of some sort. From time to time he would arrive and shine a light in her eyes and while asking her questions would converse easily with her. Though what he made of her answers she could not tell. More often than not, whether it was because of whatever was wrong with her or because of the strong medication that was administered, she invariably floated off to sleep mid-conversation.

Her other frequent male visitor was about ten years younger than the other man. That man was about thirty-five or thirty-six, was equally tall, but was trimmer, fitter-looking. But he did not ask questions. Instead he would come and sit by her bedside and would sometimes quietly chat to her or sit silently by her bed. She went to sleep on him too.

Days passed without her being aware of anything very much. They called her Claire; she supposed somebody must know her and had told them who she was. She had blurred recall of moments of panic, moments of near hysteria, before some injection or other would float her away to calmer waters. She had a hazy recollection of being transferred from one ward to another, and then of being moved from there to another hospital entirely—but while she was in a sea of new faces and nurses she did not recognise the consultant and the other man were still constant visitors.

Then one morning she awakened and for the first time did not so soon drift away again. This time she stayed awake. While she still had no memory, and her head still felt a little muzzy, she felt stronger and, with relief, as if she was ready to join the land of the living.

'Where am I?' she asked the pretty nurse who at that moment came in to check on her.

'Roselands.' The nurse answered straight away. And, obviously aware that that piece of information meant nothing to her, 'It's a private clinic. You were transferred here two days ago—a sure sign you're on the mend.'

'My name's Claire?'

'Claire Farley,' the nurse replied without hesitation, clearly knowing all that there was to know about her patient.

'What happened to me? How…?'

'You were in a road traffic accident. You're badly bruised and were in a coma for a short while, but you've come through and have nothing life-threatening wrong with you. You've had a few stitches in your right thigh—all out now—and cuts and grazes to your right arm which didn't require stitches, and some muscle trauma, but otherwise,' the nurse added with a comforting smile, 'no bones broken.'

'Is my head all right?' Claire asked, feeling panic rising but finding she had a little more control than she'd had previously and managing to hold her panic down. 'I can't remember…'

'Your head's fine,' the nurse hurriedly assured her. 'If there's a test around we know about, you've had it. You've been X-rayed, scanned and, given that the whole of you received one almighty jolt when you went flying through the air, I can promise you, you've been left with no permanent damage.'

'But I can't remember who I am.' A hint of panic had started to creep into her tones.

'Try to relax,' the nurse soothed. 'I'm Beth Orchard, by the way. As I've mentioned, you were in a coma for a brief while, and your poor head has decided it wants a rest. Now, the sooner you can start to relax, the sooner your memory will return.' From where Claire was viewing it, she seemed to have been having one enormous long rest just lately. 'Now, is there anything I can get for you?'

Claire looked around the room. There was the most beautiful flower arrangement in one corner of the room, and another small posy on her bedside table, plus a basket of fruit. 'I seem to have everything,' she replied, and wanted to ask more questions, but somehow, even in her highly anxious state, did not seem to have any energy.

Beth Orchard went away, and Claire began to experience emotions of hysteria starting to rise—everything was a blank, a brick wall—and she just could not get through it. She pushed and pushed, but there was nothing there.

'Claire Farley,' she said out loud, fighting for calm, but the name sounded alien on her tongue.

Just when panic was on the rise again, however, the door opened and the consultant she seemed to know as Dr Phipps entered. Though, since he was a consultant surgeon, she hazily recalled the nursing staff respectfully addressed him as Mr Phipps. 'How's the head?' he enquired, coming to the bed and casting a professional eye over her.

'Everything's black. There's no light. Nothing there,' she replied, telling him that which was the more important to her.

'You need rest,' he said confidently.

'So Nurse Orchard said.'

'Try your best not to worry,' Mr Phipps suggested.

'How long? How long will it be before I get my memory back?' Claire asked anxiously, and, more essentially, '*Will* I get it back?'

'It could return any time at all now,' he replied. 'If it's purely a case of a knock on your head, your memory might come trotting back within the next day or week or two. Just rest and...'

'If?' Claire questioned, discovering she had an intelligence of a sort that wanted to know more. 'Is that an implication that there might be more to my condition than a knock on the head?'

He hesitated briefly, but gave her the straight answer she

required. 'Sometimes when a person has endured some kind of enormous emotional stress, to an extent that the person just cannot take any more, the brain decides enough is enough, and for a while decides to block everything out.'

'Do you think that may have happened to me?'

'It is possible for the two to come together—the bang on the head and the overloaded emotional trauma—but, from eyewitness accounts of you having an argument with a moving vehicle, I believe at this stage that your accident is the culprit.'

Claire accepted that. She had no choice. Mr Phipps was a clever man, and she trusted him. 'My family?' she asked. 'They know I'm here?' He did not answer. 'I do have a family? Perhaps I don't?'

'When I said you were to rest, I meant it.' He smiled. 'Let that poor brain of yours take it easy for a while.'

She felt exhausted suddenly, as if any fight she had in her had just been flattened. 'All right,' she agreed, and closed her eyes.

She had no idea how long she slept, but awoke to find that she was alone. She was feeling anxious and disturbed again, and terribly lethargic too. She looked down at her right hand resting on top of the bedcover and noticed, quite incidentally, that while the fingers on that hand were slender, and actually quite narrow and dainty, her nails must have grown while she was in hospital—they could definitely do with a trim.

Hope began to fill her that her memory might soon come back, because, somehow, she just knew that as a general rule she did not care for her nails to be overlong.

She took her left hand from beneath the covers to inspect the nails on that hand—and went rocketing out from her feeling of lethargy when, with disbelieving amazement, she saw she was wearing the most beautiful diamond solitaire on her engagement finger. She was engaged! Engaged to be married!

Who to? Not that dark-haired man, the other tall one? She dimly remembered that he had been sitting by her bed yesterday—or had it been the day before?

She started to panic again and looked feverishly around for a bell so she might ring for a nurse. Before she could do so, though, she managed to gain a modicum of control, sufficient anyway for her to realise that the nursing staff must have plenty of better things to do than rush in to pat her hand and say There, there.

What could anyone do that wasn't being done already? Panic began to rise again that she couldn't remember being engaged. Could remember nothing. Suppose she never regained her memory?

Just when she was having a hard time repressing a fresh urge to ring the bell anyway, she heard someone at the door of her room. A second later that someone came in. Any relief she might have felt, however, that she might have company which might ease her panic, quickly evaporated when she saw that the person who had entered was the tall, dark-haired man whom she thought she might be engaged to.

'Am I that scary?' he asked, over at her bed in a couple of strides, causing her to realise she must have been looking extremely alarmed. He smiled then, and she began to feel a touch better.

'Am I—am I engaged to you?' she asked.

He went over to bring a chair nearer to her bed and sat down beside her. 'It was I who put that ring on your finger,' he answered gently.

She stared at him. Surely to be engaged to him must mean that she loved him, and yet looking at him she felt nothing— except relief that he hadn't staked his claim by kissing her in greeting. 'I don't know your name,' she told him. He had steady grey eyes—she did not seem able to stop looking at him.

'Tye,' he supplied, and, with a most superb grin, 'Allow me to introduce myself. Tyerus Kershaw at your service.'

She found she was smiling. 'I think I could like you,' she said, quite without thinking—and swiftly realised, Oh, the poor man. It was her love he wanted, not her liking. 'I'm sorry,' she apologised quickly. 'I don't seem to know very much. Though...' She hesitated.

'You've remembered something?' Suddenly he was looking very serious, stern almost.

She shook her head. 'I noticed my hands for the first time today. My nails need cutting. I've a feeling, in fact I'm sure, I don't normally have them this long. I—' She broke off as she all at once realised something else. 'I don't know what I look like!' she said on a gasp. And, looking at him earnestly, 'Am I plain?' she asked hurriedly.

His mouth curved upwards. 'You are beautiful,' he assured her. 'Quite beautiful.'

'Are you just saying that because you're engaged to me and beauty is in the eye of the beholder?' She did not wait for him to reply this time, finding instead that she urgently needed to know what she looked like. 'Is there a mirror anywhere?'

For answer he left his chair and went and opened the door to the small adjoining bathroom. 'Your consultant tells me he wants you to sit out of bed for a short while this afternoon,' he announced. And, coming back to her, while she was taking on board that he must have seen Mr Phipps very recently, Tye leaned down, pulled back the covers and, taking care not to hurt her bruised body, gently collected her in his arms. 'We'll do a trial run,' he said conspiratorially.

To feel through the thinness of her nightdress his strong all-male arms so securely about her caused warm colour to flare to her cheeks. She was thankful that she seemed decently enough clad, and was never more grateful that her bedwear, being an expensive-looking silk and lace affair, was not the open-up-the-back hospital issue.

Her blush had barely subsided, however, when she found that the stranger she was engaged to had carried her into the bathroom and had turned so she should see herself in the mirror above the wash basin.

'You—said—beautiful,' she commented slowly, studying the creamy complexioned blue-eyed blonde who stared solemnly back at her.

'As well as enduring cuts, abrasions and heavily bruised muscle, your whole body has been in trauma—and that's leaving aside your poor head,' Tye answered. 'You are beautiful now and you'll be absolutely stunning when you have more of your natural colour back.'

She looked from her image and into his face. More of her natural colour? Was he saying he was aware of her blush earlier? He had a nice mouth, she observed—and looked hastily away. It seemed impossible that she had exchanged kisses with this sophisticated man, this man who, probably without him even being aware of it, wore an air of knowing exactly what he wanted from life and how to get it. Yet she was engaged to him, so they must have kissed, had probably made love. Warm colour surged to her face again at that thought.

She pushed nervous fingers through her blonde hair. 'I want to go back to bed!' she said abruptly. She felt shy, shaky, and all at once not a little weepy.

He looked down at her and, she knew, must be noticing her fiery cheeks. 'Just take it easy,' he bade her kindly when without more ado he carried her from the bathroom and without fuss popped her back into her bed. 'Everything is all haywire for you at the moment, but it will get better, I promise,' he assured her as he tucked the bedclothes in around her.

'Have I always felt shy with you?' she asked, and, feeling another wave of panic start to attack, 'I don't even know that—if I was ever shy with you!' she exclaimed. 'Shouldn't I feel comfortable with you?'

'Why should you? At this stage in your recovery I must seem a perfect stranger to you.'

Claire found a smile then. 'Thank you for being so understanding.'

He smiled back. 'You're lovely,' he said, and she suddenly discovered that she *was* feeling comfortable with him.

She yawned delicately. 'I don't seem to be able to keep my eyes open for longer than ten minutes at a time,' she apologised.

'On that big hint,' he teased, 'I'll go back to my office and get some work done.'

He went. He went without kissing her goodbye, or even giving her a peck on the cheek. She was grateful to him for that. He *was* a perfect stranger to her, and she had enough going on inside emotionally without feeling his nice warm mouth against her skin.

She realised then that Tye Kershaw disturbed her more than somewhat. That was to say that from lying there in her bed with nothing very much going on in her head, after ten minutes spent with him she had gone from shy to tense and nervous, and from there to comfortable. She could still recall the feel of his strong arms about her. She had blushed twice—had she always blushed so easily?

She recalled the features of the young woman in the mirror: wide blue eyes, dainty nose and a pleasant mouth. She looked to be somewhere in her early twenties. She must ask Tye... She fell asleep.

She awoke with her thoughts disjointed. Tye had been going back to his office. He had obviously taken time out to come and visit her. She had no idea what work he did. She must ask him. How had he known she was in hospital? She supposed she must have failed to turn up for some date with him. Perhaps she had been close to the appointed place, and he had heard of the accident and had come looking for her. Tye...

Tye went out of her head when a nurse brought her the

shoulder bag that had been found at the scene of the accident. It was of good quality, but as Claire examined the contents, a lipstick, a compact, a purse, she saw nothing that triggered any memory.

Over the following week she made rapid progress in her recovery. So that Mr Phipps, whose visits were less frequent now, was talking of discharging her. She was so much better, she knew that, but she still had some way to go before she regained her full strength. While her memory of events prior to waking up in hospital was as blank as ever, and though she was starting to fidget about being hospital bound, the thought of leaving panicked her.

Which meant that with part of her she could not wait to leave the clinic, while another part of her dreaded the thought of departing from that which had become secure to her.

Tye came to see her most days, but not always since his work involved him travelling about the country and occasionally staying out of London overnight.

Up until then she had not known where in England she was, and only then realised she must be in London. It was Tye who filled in a few other blanks. But—and she gathered it was so as not to confuse her by telling her everything at once—there was still a very great deal that she did not know.

She had asked him about his work, and he had been quite open about that. 'I'm an independent business analyst,' he had replied. His company was called Kershaw Research and Analysis, and from the little he had told her she was able to glean that he had a team of first-class troubleshooters working for him. She had also gathered that his company was in constant demand by businesses that needed their top-class analytical skills to delve into why and where the problem of pending failure or collapse threatened and lay.

Claire would have liked to know more, but Tye seemed to think he had told her enough. So she had asked him what work she did. He had told her she was between jobs at the moment, and somehow, when meaning to press him on what work did she normally do anyway, he had gone on to another subject.

'How did we meet?' was another of the questions she had asked, to which she had not received a very full answer. Though she understood the reason for that. Apparently their romance had been one of those love-at-first-sight romances. But perhaps aware, or maybe even following some kind of instruction from Mr Phipps, of trying not to strain her emotionally, Tye had steered the conversation elsewhere.

And in truth she could not say she was sorry. It did not exactly embarrass her to think of the loving relationship she must have had with Tye, but, recalling yet again his strong arms holding her that time, she could not deny she felt quite emotionally muddled up inside when she thought of it.

She waited on Sunday, expecting all day that Tye would pay her a visit, but when eight o'clock that evening arrived and he had still not come she knew that he would not be coming. And she wanted him to come.

She realised that being his own boss meant that he worked all sorts of hours, weekends too. Perhaps he was working outside of London somewhere and still had work to do. Which was a pity. She was on the point of being discharged from the clinic and had not the slightest idea of where she lived. Nor, she had discovered, did any of the nursing staff know where she lived. Or, if they did know, no one was telling.

She had been sitting out of bed for quite some while, but as her anxiety began to mount, she decided to get back into bed. She was very stiff in places—her muscles would recover in due time, she had been assured—but while admittedly not breaking any speed records, her body ached as she made it into bed and sat there pondering. What did she do now?

She had asked Tye about her family and he had replied

that her parents were travelling, touring somewhere in North America. He had thought—if she was in agreement, and since her memory loss was not life-threatening—that he would not try and contact them and break the holiday they had looked forward to for so long.

Since she would not know them even if they were located and did rush back, Claire was in complete agreement. She surmised she must be an only child. What did bother her now, though, was the thought that she could not possibly occupy a bed at the clinic for much longer; it would be the height of selfishness if someone more needy were waiting for a bed. But nor did she fancy leaving the clinic, where a nurse or cleaner or someone would bustle in every hour or so, to go home to an empty house and stare blankly at the walls all day.

That was if she lived in a house. For all she knew she might have a small flat somewhere, a bedsit, even. Her feelings of anxiety went up another notch. Then suddenly, just when she felt desperate for someone to talk to, the door opened—and Tye came in.

'Oh, I'm so pleased to see you!' she cried, and, embarrassed that she was all at once feeling quite tearful, looked away from him.

'Hey, what's this?' he asked lightly, and, coming quickly over to her, he perched on the edge of her bed and placed an arm about her shoulders. Then he placed his other hand to the side of her face and made her look at him. 'What's wrong?' he asked gently—and at his tone, his touch, she went all marshmallowy inside.

She swallowed, desperate not to cry. 'Mr Phipps says, given that I shall have to come back for a check-over, that I'm almost ready to leave here.'

Tye Kershaw studied her face for some silent seconds. What he was trying to read in her eyes she had no idea, but she was totally unprepared for his quiet, 'Like—tomorrow.'

'L... tomorrow?' She quickly caught on. 'I can go home tomorrow? You've seen Mr Phipps?'

'I managed to have a few words with him on the phone,' Tye answered, and smiled a smile she was beginning to love when he added, 'So what worries you about that to cause those big, beautiful, astonishingly blue eyes to shine so unhappily?'

'I don't know where I live!' she mumbled helplessly.

'Oh, my dear,' he crooned, his arm tightening soothingly across her shoulders.

'Where *do* I live?' she asked urgently. 'Nobody seems able to tell me.' She looked at him expectantly, and he seemed about to speak but hesitated. And all at once Claire suddenly thought she knew the reason for his hesitation; thought she understood. 'I live with you,' she said. 'We live together, don't we?' And, as the implication of that abruptly rocketed into her head, so scarlet colour flared in her face. 'Do I—sleep with you?' she asked croakily.

'Shh...' Tye hushed her, and, as if to make their relationship less personal, he took his arm from about her shoulders and moved away from the bed. His expression was hidden for a few seconds while he took up the visitor's chair and brought it over to the bed. Then, perhaps so she should not have to strain to look up at him, he casually lowered his length on to it and, looking across, sent her a calm, encouraging smile. 'You are making excellent progress,' he said. 'But you're a long, long way from being fit enough to share a bed with anyone. And apart from that,' he added, his smile becoming a most fascinating grin, 'I have given Mr Phipps my most solemn undertaking that, even should you beg me to make love to you when I take you home, I will not.' She laughed then. It was a good sound, her laughter. She felt as if it was a long time since she had laughed out loud, or inwardly either.

'Your laughter is as lovely as your voice,' Tye remarked lightly, his eyes on her face, and it was almost as if he had never heard her laugh before—she supposed it *had* been a long time.

She forgot that when something he had just said came back to her, and in that instant she became serious. 'You said you were taking me home? Where?' she asked quickly. 'Where is home? Here—in London?'

He shook his head. 'A village in Hertfordshire,' he answered. 'Mr Phipps believes you should have rest and quiet, peace to fully recover. He thinks you'll rest much better there than in my London apartment.'

'You have two homes?' she questioned, having formed the opinion that Mr Phipps would prefer her to receive information slowly, but wanting to know everything at once.

'I recently inherited Grove House from my grandmother,' Tye responded.

'Have I been there before?'

He shook his head. 'It will be a new beginning for you,' he replied. 'You know no one there and no one will know you.' He gave her an encouraging look. 'So you won't have to worry about whether or not to say hello to someone you pass in the street.'

She hadn't thought of that. Although, since she was only recently on her feet, she doubted she could walk a hundred yards without collapsing. To take a walk outside had not featured largely in her thoughts.

'Your grandmother died?' she asked, some quirky side of her brain hopping on to that thought.

'She died a few months ago.'

'I'm sorry.' Claire suddenly felt she had been insensitive to ask the question. 'Did I know your grandmother?'

'You never met her,' he replied, adding encouragingly, 'You'll like Shipton Ash; I'm sure of it.'

'That's where Grove House is?'

'It's only a small village. A shop, a pub, and a few other properties scattered about.'

'I'll live there on my own?' she asked, while not wanting

to live with Tye as though she were his wife starting to feel a little worried about leaving the clinic, with no memory, to spend each day and night in some strange house by herself.

'I'll be there as much as I can,' Tye promised her. And, at her quick nervous look, 'Don't worry, you'll have your own room. And when I'm not there Jane Harris, my grandmother's former housekeeper-cum-nurse will come and stay with you.'

Claire's eyes widened slightly. 'You've arranged all this? While I've been—idling here, you've been busy arranging all this for my welfare?'

'I've led a pretty selfish life,' Tye informed her. 'Indulge me.'

'I don't believe you have a selfish bone in your body,' she denied. 'Your visits to me have been constant...' Her voice trailed away. Was that what you did when you loved someone—looked after their welfare, smoothed their path when things got a touch rocky? 'Do you love me?' she asked abruptly, and, quickly after that thought, 'Do I love you?' she asked.

Grey eyes stared into her deeply blue ones. Unexpectedly her heart had started to pound at the thought that this extremely attractive and sophisticated man might be about to tell her that he loved her, but he did nothing of the kind, but said instead, 'I think for the time being you and I should just be friends, and nothing more than that.'

'Oh,' she murmured. And, with either her pride or her intelligence at work, 'You'd like your engagement ring back?' She went to remove it from her finger, but Tye stretched out a hand and placed it over her hands, staying her movements.

'That's not what I'm suggesting at all!' he stated. 'What I'm saying is that for the time being, until you are fully well, our engagement becomes a platonic affair.'

'A platonic engagement,' she echoed, more to get over

the tingling kind of sensation the touch of his warm hand over hers was causing. But, when she did think of what he was saying, 'I like it,' she said, and Tye let go of her hand and stood up.

'I'll leave you to get some rest,' he commented. 'You've an exhausting day in front of you tomorrow.'

'Clothes!' she exclaimed, having a last-minute panic; she didn't really want to make the journey to Grove House in her nightwear.

'All arranged,' he assured her. 'Get some rest,' he repeated, and left her.

Claire was awake for ages after he had gone. She looked at her engagement ring. Platonic engagement. The two words brought a smile to her face. He was nice, her platonic fiancé. She felt she liked him, and would have done so even if she had not known him prior to losing her memory.

Mr Phipps had said her memory would return any day now. She wished it would hurry up. Not only on her own account, but Tye's too, she realised. She wanted to know more of him as well. Wanted to remember about him and their relationship. What they did, where they went, what they talked about. She wanted to recall their favourite places, their favourite restaurant.

She again thought of the feel of his strong arms around her that day she had wanted to know what she looked like—and wanted to remember their more intimate moments together. She was pretty sure, Tye being such a virile-looking man and everything—not to mention that she had lived with him—that they must have been lovers. And yet she had no memory of sharing herself with him. And Tye? He seemed in no hurry to share so much as a kiss with her. All of which made him a rather superb platonic fiancé. For the first time since her accident she went to sleep with a smile playing about her mouth.

It had gone two the next afternoon before she saw Tye again. He had to work, she knew that, and she tried to be patient, but while a percentage of her felt hesitant and even a touch reluctant to leave the security of Roselands clinic, there was a greater part of her that wanted to make that journey to Grove House. Perhaps once she was on the outside of hospital life, living a normal kind of existence, her memory would come rushing back.

Tye arrived carrying a suitcase—the contents of which, as well as some expensive-looking underwear, included jeans, trousers and tops. All of which appeared to be new. Perhaps he had packed only the newest additions to her wardrobe.

'I couldn't have been wearing any of this when I was brought into hospital!' she commented slowly. It seemed to her that if her body had taken such an assault that she'd been unconscious for days, some of what she had been wearing at the time must have suffered some snag or tear at the very least.

'Apart from your shoes, you weren't,' Tye agreed. 'Not to dwell on the subject too much, you were completely out of it, making it impossible for you to tell anyone if you hurt more in one place than another. Rather than do more damage in getting you out of your clothes, the solution was to cut your clothes from you so the doctors could quickly trace the source of the blood and assess the extent of your injuries.'

'Everyone put in a lot of effort for me, didn't they?' she said gratefully.

And was grateful again, to Tye this time, that, when he must have seen her at some time totally without her clothes, and might even have helped her out of them occasionally for all she knew, he said, 'I'll get a nurse to help you get changed.'

It was Beth Orchard who came and helped her to dress, and, having thought she would need very little assistance, Claire was amazed at how weak she felt and how much help she needed.

'Lying in bed will do that for you,' Beth Orchard said cheerfully, even though Claire had sat out of bed daily and for progressively longer periods.

Claire thanked everyone for their splendid care and, holding on to Tye's arm, she left the clinic. It was a mild October day, and it was wonderful to be out in the air, a light wind fanning her face and hair.

Tye walked slowly. She was glad that he did. Incredibly, she felt exhausted by the time they reached his long sleek Jaguar. 'In you get,' he said lightly, without fuss helping her into the passenger seat.

It was a joy to be out, to be a human being as opposed to a patient. She wanted to savour everything, and looked about her as they left the car park hoping that perhaps something, any little thing, might trigger off some spark of memory.

But, look around as she did, she saw nothing that spurred a memory, and slowly her eyelids began to grow heavy and she fell asleep. She woke up once, glanced at the man by her side; he glanced back, they smiled at each other—and she went to sleep again.

She awakened just in time to see a sign saying Shipton Ash. 'We're there!' she exclaimed, and unexpectedly started to feel worried. 'Will Jane Harris be there?' she asked anxiously.

If Tye noticed her suddenly anxious state he gave no indication, but replied calmly, 'I hope so. I could murder a cup of tea.'

Claire felt instantly better again. 'I'm sorry,' she apologised, perfectly aware that, while he was quite capable of making his own tea, he was doing his best to ease for her this time of leaving the security of the clinic. Perhaps Mr Phipps had warned she might feel a trifle agitated from time to time.

Abruptly then she forgot all about how she was feeling, for Tye was stopping the car and was getting out to open a pair of high and wide iron gates. Astonished, having for no particular reason supposed Grove House to be a small cottage kind of a house, she saw at the end of an avenue of beautiful trees that lined the drive the most elegant building that could have been quite appropriately named manor house.

She opened her mouth to say as much as Tye got back into the car. But as she looked from him down the long tree-lined drive, suddenly, without warning, and as if from far off, she heard herself say, 'My mother loved trees. She—' Claire broke off, turning sharply to Tye, switching her gaze away from the trees to him, her mouth falling open in shock.

Immediately his hands came out and he caught a firm hold of her upper arms. 'You're all right,' he assured her quietly, calmly. Then questioned, 'You've remembered—?'

'Only that!' she cut in, feeling totally shaken. Then, urgently, her eyes growing wide, 'I said that my mother loved trees. *Loved!*' she emphasised. 'You said my parents were on holiday in—' She broke off, her breath catching. 'Is my mother dead?' she asked faintly. 'Is she?' she asked urgently. 'Tye, please tell me.'

CHAPTER TWO

TYE looked into her troubled blue eyes, his expression controlled. 'Let's get you inside the house,' he said after a moment, and started the car's motor.

Her head had begun to ache. She subsided back into her seat. She had no idea where that memory had sprung from, but it was there, as fact—her mother *had* loved trees.

Jane Harris must have been on the lookout for them because she had the front door of Grove House open as they drew up outside. She was a well-covered woman in her late fifties who beamed a smile and stood back as Tye, with an arm around Claire, helped her into the wide hall.

He introduced them, adding, 'The journey has been a bit much for Claire. I'll take her straight up.'

'Your rooms are all ready for you,' Jane Harris replied. 'Shall I bring some tea?'

'Would you, Jane?' he accepted, and, turning to Claire, commented, 'You're never going to make those stairs under your own steam,' then, as if she weighed nothing, he picked her up in his arms and made for the wide and elegant staircase.

'I can walk!' she protested, but owned she did feel a mite exhausted.

Once more held against his chest as—effortlessly, it seemed—he carried her to one of the upstairs room, Claire tried to dispel the unsettling feeling that something was wrong—something was very, very wrong.

In the room Tye set her down on the bed, moving her so that she was sitting leaning against the pillows with her feet on the bed. But even as he was straightening up she was asking, 'Tell me about my mother, Tye?'

24

He looked into her distressed eyes and was silent for a second or two, and then, 'The truth is, little one,' he answered, 'I don't know anything about your mother.'

'You never met her?'

'I never did.'

'But... But you said my parents were on hol—' She broke off, her intelligence at work. 'Did you and Mr Phipps think it better I should think my parents were on holiday rather than I should know my mother was dead?' she asked.

'He didn't want you to be concerned about absolutely anything,' Tye replied. 'And, quite honestly, I think you've coped with more than enough for one day. I'll get your case, and Jane can help you into bed.'

'What if I remember something else?' Claire asked, starting to panic suddenly.

'I'm not going far, only out to the car,' he assured her, and had not been gone for more than a minute when Jane Harris arrived with a tray of tea.

Claire took to Jane Harris, who asked her to call her by her first name, and they were sipping tea when Tye returned with the case he had brought to the clinic.

'I'll leave you to it,' he said. 'I'll—'

'You're not leaving...' Claire cut in hurriedly, and, feeling slightly shamefaced that he had become her anchor and that she should feel so panicky at the thought of him going '...yet,' she added.

He smiled. 'I've nothing pressing to get back to London for.'

Jane unpacked her case when he had gone, and helped her into bed. When her eyelids started to droop, Jane went quietly away and left her to rest.

But Claire could not rest; her head would not let her. She knew that her mother had had a feeling for trees, and that her mother was dead. Those two scraps of knowledge spun round and around in her brain. So that by the time Jane brought her an early-evening meal Claire was feeling close to being spent of all energy.

When Jane had gone, from innate good manners Claire attempted to eat as much of the casserole Jane had been good enough to prepare as she could. But Claire had scant appetite. She started to fret that she was putting everyone to a lot of bother.

She contemplated getting out of bed and carrying her used dishes downstairs, and was just pondering the possibility of the tray and her shaky self arriving in the kitchen in one piece when Jane returned.

'Not hungry?' she enquired, as with a professional glance at Claire's slight figure Jane picked up the bed tray. 'I can see I shall have my work cut out trying to put a few pounds on you,' she added lightly.

'I'm sorry,' Claire apologised, aware that for all she curved in the right places, and was not lacking in the bosom department, still the same she was on the thin side of slender. 'The casserole was delicious.' She thanked the woman who could add first-rate cook to her list of other skills.

'I'll just take your tray downstairs and tidy up a bit, then I'll be off.' She smiled warmly. 'Now, is there anything you need before I go?'

'You're not staying the night?' Claire asked in a flash of alarm.

'Mr Kershaw will be here,' Jane quickly assured her, and was all sympathy as she straightened the bedcovers and soothed, 'Try not to worry. It's only natural you should suffer pangs of insecurity from time to time. But—' her tone brightened '—between us we'll get you right.'

Claire survived her small attack of panic, and found a smile. 'You're a nurse as well as a four-star cook,' she remarked.

'Fully trained nurse and a muddle-along cook,' Jane laughed.

'You didn't care for nursing?'

'Loved it,' Jane replied. 'Until my back went. But I was lucky,' she went on cheerfully. 'Just when I knew I was going to have to look for an alternative occupation I heard old Mrs Kershaw needed a housekeeper—knowledge of nursing an advantage. She wasn't ill then, but frail, and with an ulcer that took for ever to heal.' She paused to give a chubby grin. 'And, as usual, I'm talking too much.'

Why, when she had done little that day, she should suddenly feel tired again was a mystery to Claire, but no sooner had Jane gone than she seemed unable to keep her eyes open.

She awoke with a start to find a tall man bending over her bed—and, as an almighty fear shrieked through her, *'Go away!'* she screamed in fear. 'Don't you dare come in here!' she yelled, rocketing upright, using what strength she had to leap horrified out of bed.

The man pulled back from the bed and made as if to come after her, but he stopped, frozen in his tracks when he saw the look of absolute horror on her face. 'My dear, it's...'

And suddenly, hearing him speak, seeing his face clearly now that he was no longer bending over her, so she recognised Tye, her fiancé. She drew a long shuddering gasp of breath, realising that his face must have been in shadow until she had moved. 'Oh, Tye,' she cried, thoroughly ashamed. 'I didn't know it was you.' With that, her legs weak, she dropped heavily on to the edge of the bed, her face ashen.

With the trauma of the moment over, Tye came round to her side of the bed and, seating himself next to her, took her into his arms. 'You're all right, sweetheart,' he said gently. 'I'm here. Nothing's going to harm you.'

She drew another fractured breath. 'Did someone harm me? Some man?' she asked, raising her head to look at him, her eyes troubled.

Tye studied her for long moments, 'I don't know,' he answered, his eyes not leaving her face.

'Mr Phipps said my loss of memory might be the result of my accident, but that sometimes a memory loss occurs if someone is trying to blot out something emotional. It can sometimes be both.'

'So I believe,' Tye replied.

'He told you the same?'

'I wanted to know all there was to know.'

Claire expected that he did. Tye was that sort of man. She gave a shaky sigh, was all at once aware that she was trembling, and realised that Tye must be aware of it too, for he held her quietly against him for some while.

Then slowly, as she began to recover from whatever unknown demons were in her past, Claire suddenly became conscious of the scantiness of her attire. Her nightdress was blue this time, bringing out the lovely deep blue colour of her eyes. One strap had fallen down her arm, and as she pulled back from Tye she saw that the silk material left very little to the imagination. She shivered unexpectedly.

'You're cold,' Tye said, smiling at her as he drew back, his eyes scanning over her. She glanced down, following his brief tour of her person, and went scarlet as she observed the swell of her breasts with the hardened peaks clearly outlined by the thinness of the material.

'I'm sorry,' she said for no reason, and their eyes met.

'Well, at least you're a better colour,' Tye teased, and she thought she knew why she had loved him. 'Just in case you're heading for a bit of shock—not to mention that it's nearly midnight,' he went on, his teasing manner falling away, 'I think we'll get you back into bed.'

In no time she was in bed, with Tye sitting in a chair next to her. He stayed with her for quite some while, conversing on various subjects, but mindful that she had no memory.

He commented lightly on Jane's delicious casserole, and Claire replied that the good thing about casseroles was that you could prepare them and then forget about them—a boon on a busy day.

'How did I know that?' she exclaimed as soon as the words were out. 'Was I some sort of a cook?'

'You never were just a pretty face,' Tye answered easily. And, looking at her, and plainly judging that she was not going to go into shock, 'Will you be all right if I leave you?' he asked.

'Of course,' she answered without hesitation.

'I'm just along the landing if you need me,' he informed her. 'I'll leave my door open. Give me a shout if—'

'Oh, Tye!' she exclaimed helplessly, and guessed then that, apart from her feeling of horror earlier, Jane must have told him of her feelings of alarm and insecurity at the thought of being alone that night. 'I'm sorry to be such a nuisance. You must be wanting to get back to London...'

'Now, why would I want to do that when my best girl's here?' he cut in lightly. Was she his best girl? It made her feel a little more secure to think so, she had to admit. 'Don't forget, I'm just along the landing,' he said, and was heading out of the room when she stopped him.

'Tye!' she called. He halted, turning, and from nowhere she found herself blurting out, 'Tye, would you kiss me?'

'I...'

'Sorry!' she swiftly exclaimed, then added, 'I seem to be for ever apologising,' and explained, 'It's just that I've forgotten what your kisses are like, and...'

'You're a glutton for punishment,' he drawled, and, with an exaggerated sigh that made her laugh, came back to the bed. 'You promise not to have your wicked way with me?' he questioned mock-toughly.

'You have my word, sir,' she said, and Tye bent down to her. A moment later his lips touched hers and she was on the receiving end of a warm but chaste kiss.

'All right?' Tye asked as he drew back, his eyes searching hers, almost as if he suspected some man might have at-

tacked her and she wanted to heal—whatever the unknown
scars—with a kiss from someone she trusted.

While it was true that her heart was racing to beat the
band, and that she was experiencing the almost uncontrol-
lable urge to throw her arms around Tye and beg for another, perhaps less chaste kiss, Claire felt just then that she
had never felt so right inside.

'Absolutely,' she answered, feeling strangely light-headed
from the touch of his lips on her. 'Goodnight, Tye.'

He looked down at her approvingly. 'Sleep tight,' he bade
her, and went quietly from her room.

She did sleep tight. But, perhaps because she had slept
quite soundly before midnight, she was awake very early.
Awake and suddenly feeling better than she had been feeling
in a long while. Her body had more or less healed, her head
was taking a little longer—so why was she lying in bed?

It was still early, still dark outside, but Claire was suddenly certain that she had led a very busy life. It seemed to
go totally against something in her to lie there idle when
she should be up and about and doing something.

There appeared to be nothing very much that she could
do, though, and she was aware that she was still regaining
her strength. But, was she to lie there for the next couple
of hours, waiting for Jane to perhaps arrive and bring her a
cup of tea?

Claire thought of Tye, who was 'just along the landing',
and wondered how long it was since anyone had brought
him a cup of tea in bed. Then she realised that perhaps,
before her accident, she had made him tea and taken it to
his bedside. Perhaps they had made love…

She drew her thoughts hastily away from such subjects,
even as her cheeks grew hot as she recalled his superb
mouth over hers last night.

As if to escape such thoughts, she got out of bed and
decided it was time to make more of an effort. So far she
had not been allowed to take a bath without someone ac-

companying her. She would start by taking a bath on her own.

She was already acquainted with the adjoining bathroom, but was astounded to find how little strength she had. Even the simple procedure of bending over the bath, securing the plug and turning on the taps caused her to need to sit on the bathroom stool while she waited for the bath to fill.

Five minutes later, however, she lay resting in the water and was starting to feel extremely proud of herself. Gone were the days of someone escorting her while she bathed. She had managed on her own—she would not have to wait for Jane to arrive.

She soaped herself, noticing that she still had traces of bruising in places. She realised then just how astonishingly lucky she had been not to break any bones when the accident had happened. Even now—and she owned she had lost all sense of time but it must be weeks later—her body was still feeling a little creaky in places. She rinsed the lovely perfumed lather away and, feeling tired again, rested in the water, letting her thoughts drift.

She thought about her mother and wondered about her father. Had her mother died recently or a long, long time ago? Had her parents been devoted to each other? Or maybe they had been divorced and... It was no good; her head was beginning to ache again. There was a barrier there and it just seemed impossible to get through it.

Claire went on to think about the way she had reacted when she had awoken last night and found Tye bending over her—probably checking to see if she was asleep. Oh, the poor man. He had been so good—and she had screamed at him for his trouble.

Had some man attacked her? She abruptly turned away from the question. She did not want to know, and for once she was glad to have no memory.

But demons seemed to be all at once tormenting her, and hurriedly, with more speed than thought, she leapt out of the bath—only to find that instead of landing on her feet she had landed in a heap on the floor.

For a moment she was too shaken to try to get up. But as she started to get herself back together again she was staggered to discover that a stitched, grazed and badly bruised body, plus some days spent comatose and more days of just lying in bed, had left her feeling shatteringly debilitated! She hurt when she tried to move too. But a few minutes later she used what energy she could find to pick herself up and make it to the bathroom stool.

Seconds, perhaps minutes, ticked by when all she was capable of doing was just sitting there. She felt battered, bruised and utterly exhausted, and was more concerned just then with finding some strength from somewhere than with the fact that she needed to dry herself.

Then someone knocked on the bathroom door. Oh, thank goodness. Jane. Claire's spirits lifted. Only it wasn't Jane. It was Tye's voice that came through the wood panelling. 'I'm not too happy about you taking a bath on your own,' he called, and Claire, with a start, realised he must have heard the water running in the plumbing system.

'I'm certainly not inviting you to join me!' she called back sharply, finding that she did not care to be discovered naked, and that, while the rest of her seemed to be incapacitated, there was nothing wrong with her tongue.

'I'm concerned in case you have a dizzy bout!' Tye returned shortly.

She did not care for his tone. 'I'm not the dizzy type!' replied she who had not a clue as to what type she was.

'You...' he began toughly, but checked, and then, more evenly, reminded her, 'You've been ill.'

'I shall feel a whole lot better when you've gone!' she retorted, and knew she was far from being herself. She was cranky, pathetically weak—and he who had been nothing but good to her did not deserve her spleen. She could only imagine that it could not be part of her normal way of life to sit naked, having a conversation with someone on the other side of a door, and that some kind of confused modesty was pushing her. 'Are you still there?' she asked, less sharply, starting to feel ashamed of herself.

'I'll stay here while you get out,' he replied.

'I am out,' she answered, and was suddenly feeling totally used up and miserable.

'Are you all right?' he asked, when seconds had passed and there were no sounds of movement.

'Of course,' she replied. 'I...' She went to stand—and was appalled that her legs felt all wobbly. 'Is—is Jane around?' she asked, trying to sound casual but with weak tears coming to her eyes.

Those tears did not fall; they were stifled by the shock she felt to hear Tye open the bathroom door. She stared at him in a stunned moment of nothing happening. Then, as she glimpsed him take in her seated and damp naked body, so she bent forward, as if hoping to hide from his view the nakedness of her breasts.

But she had no need to worry on that score, she soon saw, for in one glance Tye seemed to take in the whole situation. And while she was still cowering there, stunned, he had grabbed up a warm fluffy towel from the heated towel rail and, draping it across her shoulders, tucked it around her.

She immediately started to feel a shade better. 'Is Jane coming today?' she asked, with no clear reason other than that, oddly, weak tears were again pressing.

'You're going to have to put up with me until later today,' he replied, and instructed, 'Sit tight. I'll be back in a minute.' True to his word, having left her only to go and collect an armful of more fluffy towels, he was back. 'Imagine I'm your best bloke,' he said, and before she could blink he had whisked one damp towel away from her and had wrapped her in a dry one. Before she knew it he was hoisting her up in his arms and was carrying her into the other room.

'I feel such a fool,' she sniffed, tears smarting again.

'You wouldn't dream of crying on me, I hope?'

'What sort of a girl do you think I am?' she rallied.

'A very lovely one,' he answered, placing her down on the edge of the bed. 'A very lovely one who's doing the very best she can in a world where everything must be completely confusing.'

'Oh, Tye!' she cried. 'I'm sorry I was so cranky earlier. I was so nasty and you are so good. I c-can't believe I have so little energy.'

'Your system has suffered one gigantic shock—nobody expects you to jump up and start doing aerobics,' he calmed her, and through the over-large towel that encased her he began to rub her dry. When that towel was damp, without the smallest fuss he whipped it from her and wrapped her in a fresh one. 'Feel snug?' he enquired. She nodded, feeling suddenly extremely tired and sleepy. 'Into bed, then,' he instructed matter of factly and, perhaps never intending her to move by herself, he lifted her, still wrapped in the dry towel, and put her into bed.

She looked up at him, and tired though she was she had to smile. 'You're a bit special, aren't you?' she mumbled, and closed her eyes.

She was already half asleep, but drifted off certain she heard him say softly, 'You're a bit special yourself, sweetheart.'

She awoke feeling hot and a little confused. The towel Tye had wrapped around her had loosened, and for a moment, as it began to come back to her why she was lying in bed naked, she could not remember where her nightdress was.

Her confused world soon righted itself when she realised it must still be in the bathroom. But she did not want to sit around in her nightdress all day. She was never going to regain her strength by just sitting around.

Her thoughts of getting out of bed, if only to sit out, as

she had at the clinic, were interrupted when someone, as if
thinking she might still be asleep, tapped lightly on her door.

'Come in!' she called, and felt embarrassed when Tye
accepted her invitation. She had a feeling that the only reason he had knocked on her door at all was to forewarn her.
Quite obviously he had no wish to invite a repetition of her
screaming at him, should she awake to find him bending
over her, as she had last night. 'What time is it?' she asked
to cover her embarrassment, while at the same time she
struggled to free herself of the over-large towel and sit up.

'A little after ten,' he answered. 'You don't—?'

'Shouldn't you be at your office?' she butted in, looking
up at his handsome face and feeling guilty that she was
keeping him from his work.

'That's one of the perks of being your own boss,' Tye
replied, coming and taking a seat on the edge of her bed. 'I
can take a day off whenever I like.'

She found him quite charming. 'But your work will suffer!' she protested.

'No, it won't,' he denied, his eyes searching her face,
assessing for himself if she had recovered from her earlier
attempt to overdo her strength. 'I've set up office in an annexe next to my grandmother's library.'

Claire stared at him wordlessly for some seconds. He had
previously told her that his grandmother had died a few
months ago, but the fact that Tye still referred to the library
in the house he had inherited as his 'grandmother's library'
seemed to state that he still thought of the house as being
his grandmother's.

In a moment of impulsive sympathy, knowing somehow
that Tye had been extremely fond of his grandmother, Claire
leaned forward to touch him. Then, as the bedclothes fell
away from her, so she went crimson.

'Oh!' she wailed, frantically grabbing at the covers to
hide her partially revealed breasts. 'Oh!' she cried again,
but felt better for being covered up—given that her shoul-

ders were exposed. 'Does everybody lose their modesty when they start to get used to people in white coats coming in to check on their progress?'

Tye smiled a friendly smile. 'You haven't lost your modesty, or even mislaid it,' he promised. 'I swear I never knew anyone to blush so prettily,' he teased. 'Or,' he added, 'so frequently.' She was still a shade pink and he, it appeared, was determined to tease her out of her discomfiture when he enquired, 'Now, what do you propose attempting for your next adventure?'

She knew he was referring to her last adventure being her attempt to get from bed, to bath and back to bed again unaided. 'I'm sorry.' She felt she owed him that. 'I would never have tried the bath had I—'

'What?' he interrupted aghast. 'You'd do me out of my rescue?'

She wasn't sure about his teasing—she could feel herself going pink again. 'Did I always blush—even before we became lovers?' she asked abruptly, and blushed again at the very thought of being lovers with him.

Tye looked as if her question had almost stumped him. Then he grinned, a heart-turning grin. 'You were ever a delight,' he said, and added briskly, 'Mr Phipps is of the opinion you should take things easy this morning and perhaps walk up and down the landing for ten minutes or so this afternoon.'

'I've done nothing but take it easy for...' Claire began to protest when suddenly something, perhaps her intelligence stirring, struck her. 'You haven't been in touch with Mr Phipps since we arrived here yesterday?'

'Why wouldn't I?' Tye asked, his expression serious. 'I had intended to anyway, when you remembered or seemed to know that your mother had a soft spot for trees. When it was obvious last night that you fear something in connection with some man or other, I felt we should have professional guidance.'

She sighed. 'I don't want to be this much trouble.'

'Good!' Tye was straight back to teasing. 'That means you're going to obey my every instruction?'

'In your dreams!' she laughed—and loved it when he laughed too. 'I think I'll get up now,' she said.

'I'd better get you something to wear.'

'I'll get dressed,' she decided.

'I thought you might,' he answered mildly, and went from the bed to root in the drawers of the chest and selected several articles of underwear that Jane had put away when she had unpacked for her. From the built-in wardrobes Tye extracted trousers and a shirt. Then he approached the bed, and Claire would swear that there was the very devil alight in his eyes when, dropping the trousers and shirt down on the bottom of the bed, he came towards her with a bra and a pair of lacy briefs. 'I'll help you,' he offered, his eyes *definitely* alive with mischief.

'I haven't lost *that* much modesty!' she erupted.

Tye gave an exaggerated sigh. 'Then I'd better go and get you some breakfast.' And he left her to take as much time as she needed in which to dress herself.

She stared at the door after he had gone, and knew that there was a great mass of information about herself which she did not know. She looked down at the beautiful engagement ring on her finger and realised that, while she might not have the smallest recall that she loved the man, what she did know was that Tye Kershaw was a man whom she most certainly liked very much.

Because she was still stiff and tender in places, as well as her movements not being as swift as she felt surely they must have been before her accident, it took her some while to get dressed. But she felt better for the effort, better for being dressed and out of bed. She was not going to return to bed in a hurry.

Breakfast was more of a brunch. 'You're trying to fatten

me up!' she accused Tye when he carried in a tray of bacon, eggs, baked beans and crisply fried bread.

'You have a marathon to run this afternoon,' he reminded her. 'Eat hearty.'

It was around three when Tye next came to her room. 'I can manage the landing on my own!' she protested, having already walked about her room a good deal—admittedly with rests in between.

'I know you can,' he replied, but didn't budge.

'I'm keeping you from your work!'

'It's all on computer—I can do it tonight,' he replied easily.

'Have I much computer experience?' she asked, her spirits suddenly plummeting that she didn't even know that much.

'Hasn't everybody?' he answered lightly. And, plainly not expecting a reply, 'Come on, Claire, time for a canter.'

Up and down the long landing they went, and for her it *was* a marathon. Not that there was anything hurried about their stroll, with Tye slowing her down when, aware he had work he must want to be getting on with, she went to move from stroll to cruise.

'Was it something I said?' he enquired, slowing her down by the simple expedient of placing a hand on her arm.

'I'll regain my strength more quickly if I push myself just that little bit,' she argued.

'Perhaps,' he conceded, determined, it seemed, not to argue. 'But—' he smiled down at her '—not today.' Looking up at him, Claire prepared to argue anyway. Then found that Tye had given her something else to think about when he went on to promise, 'If you make steady progress, we could try taking a walk outside by the end of the week.'

She instantly fell into step with him. The way she was feeling right then she knew she would be hard put to make it halfway up the long, long drive. 'It's Tuesday today?' she documented, all days having blurred into one at the clinic.

'It is,' he confirmed.

'Does Friday count as the start of the weekend?'

Tye gave her a smile that warmed her heart. 'If you behave yourself,' he agreed.

Claire was ready to attempt another length of the landing and back again, but had to admit that she was not too put out when he decided she had done enough for one day.

They parted at the door of her room and she went in, deciding to take her ease in the window seat. It was from there that she saw Jane arrive in her car, and not long afterwards the ex-nurse came to her room with a tray of sandwiches and a pot of tea. 'Just a little something to keep you going until dinner,' Jane explained—when Claire was still feeling full from brunch.

'It's a conspiracy!' she exclaimed, and Jane laughed.

'I think you probably lost a pound or two while you were in hospital,' she opined. 'Is there anything I can tempt you with for dinner?'

'You're staying on for a few hours?'

'I'm enjoying myself,' Jane replied. 'I'll be back around nine tomorrow morning, by the way. If you can stay in bed that long, I'll be here as soon as I've walked my neighbour's dog. He—my neighbour—isn't so good on his feet these days.'

Jane stayed chatting for a brief while, and after she had gone Claire rather surmised that Tye had soon had a word with Jane on the possibility of her being around at bathtime tomorrow morning.

Quite when, having transferred herself to a padded bedroom chair, her spirits began to take a nosedive, Claire could not be sure. She had been thinking along the lines of Tye's goodness, borne out by the fact that, engaged as they were, he was making not the smallest demand on her. His patience was quite astonishing, she realised, when she considered that, as intimate as they must have been in the past—as intimate as they had been now in that he had seen her in

various stages of undress—he was bothering to call in Jane
to help with her bath. Claire felt hot all over when it came
to her that for all she could remember they might well have
bathed together!

And that was the trouble. She could not remember. Push
to remember though she might, there was nothing there but
a huge blank blackness. She pushed and pushed—but nothing. It was all very well for everyone to say relax, her memory would come back. But it wouldn't; so how could she
relax?

She began to feel on edge, anxiety gnawing at her. She
got up out of her chair. She couldn't take it—this blankness,
this isolation of body and mind. She went to the door, not
knowing where she was going but feeling she would go mad
if she did not get out from there.

Out on the landing, she strove to keep her breathing even.
She was having a bit of a panic attack, that was all. She
needed something else to occupy her mind. Trying to dig
for memories that just weren't there was driving her crazy.

Claire found something else to occupy her mind when
she decided to negotiate what suddenly seemed like a mile-
long staircase. She took her time, with part of her impatient
and urging, For goodness' sake, you seem more like a hundred than twenty… Twenty-what? She didn't even know
how old she was!

Feeling desperate all of a sudden, it was only by an effort
of sheer will that she did not slump down on the stairs and
burst into tears of utter desolation, frustration and fear.

She *made* herself go on. *Made* herself go down, a step at
a time. So, OK, her body *had* felt as though it had been
flattened by some ton weight, but she was sure she did not
ache nearly so much today as she had yesterday. Positive,
that was the way forward. Stay positive.

She owned she felt close to collapse when she reached
the last three stairs. She gripped the beautiful wood banister

and was determined, given a little respite, that she was going to make it the rest of the way.

Being sure she had not made any noise in her descent, she was startled to suddenly see that Tye had just come out from one of the doors along the hall.

'What the…?' he began, and, his face like thunder, came striding towards her, his arms reaching for her as he halted at the bottom of the stairs. But, after her mammoth journey, she wasn't having that.

'No!' she yelled, and, ignoring his thunderous expression, 'I want to do it myself,' she said stubbornly.

Tye stared angrily at her, his grey assessing eyes looking hard into her deeply blue ones. There was a wealth of exasperation in his expression, but his arms did drop to his sides, and he did take a step back.

Feeling that her legs were going to give way at any moment, Claire bent her head and drew on all her reserves of strength. She peppered that strength with a helping of bravado, and, hoping he was too busy watching her feet to notice that her knuckles on the hand holding the banister were white, she negotiated the rest of the stairs.

Only when she had made it to the hall floor and was standing beside him did she look up. After such black despair, adrenalin was pumping away in her—adrenalin at her achievement. She was not sure it wasn't a hint of admiration she had glimpsed in his eyes. But, ready to drop though she might be, she had made those stairs on her own!

'Now?' Tye enquired dryly, and she knew he was asking was she ready now to accept his assistance? The alternative, she was fairly certain, was to fall flat on her face in front of him.

'Now,' she accepted, and from such a void of dark-filled hopelessness she gave a triumphant laugh as Tye bent and picked her up in his arms.

He carried her into the drawing room and deposited her

gently onto a sofa. Then, standing back, he asked, 'What am I going to do with you?'

'Don't be cross with me,' she begged. 'I was...' She stopped. He had enough to do without listening to her woes.

But, 'You were?' he insisted.

'I needed to get out of my room. Events w-were crowding in on me,' she answered, her voice on the shaky side. 'That is,' she continued after a gulp of breath, 'non-events were getting the better of me. I tried to remember something, anything, but...' her voice started to fade '...but there's nothing there.'

'Oh, my dear,' Tye murmured, sitting down beside her. 'I feel helpless to help—other than to tell you that Mr Phipps believes there's a good chance your memory is starting to stir.'

'I wish it would hurry up.'

'Hopefully it will.' Tye changed the subject. 'You were splendid with those stairs. What, I wonder, are you going to do for an encore?'

He was teasing, and she thought she could love him. 'Swing from the chandeliers?' she replied, but felt dreadful suddenly for keeping him from his work. 'Is it all right if I just sit here for a little while?' she asked.

'The change of scene will do you good.'

'But only if you go back to work,' she bargained.

'Slave-driver! Am I glad I don't work for you!' She grinned, and saw his eyes on her mouth. Then he was asking, 'Are you going to be all right if I leave you for a while?'

'Of course. I'm over whatever it was.'

He gave her hand a light squeeze and stood up. 'If you put your feet up on the sofa and rest for a while, there's a fair chance you'll be allowed to stay down for dinner.'

Without another word she took off her shoes and stretched out on the sofa. She closed her eyes, waited a moment, and then opened one eye. Tye was still there, watching her. But just before he walked away she saw his mouth pick up at the corners.

Dinner, for the most part, was a pleasant meal. Claire made it to the dining room under her own power, and enjoyed sitting at a dining table for what she realised was the first time that she could remember.

Since, however, Tye seemed to know very little about her family, and because she felt a need to absorb some knowledge of his, she asked, 'You've probably already told me, but would you tell me again about your family? Have I met any of them?'

'You're acquainted with Miles, my stepbrother, but not Paulette, his exuberant wife,' Tye replied.

'Your parents?' Claire prompted, when it seemed he had nothing to add.

'My mother left home when I was a toddler. I hardly know her.'

'Did—did your grandmother bring you up?' Claire asked, thinking it sad that he should have so little to do with his mother, but supposing, since she had gained an impression that he'd been close to his grandmother, that that lady had played a large part in his life after his mother's departure.

'I lived with her during the week. My father wanted me with him at weekends. When he remarried he insisted I live permanently with him and my stepmother.'

'The arrangement was successful?'

'Very. Anita is a little older than my father, and has a son ten years older than me. But she couldn't have been kinder had I been her son too.'

'You all got on well?'

'Extremely.'

'How lovely.' Claire smiled, not doubting that there had been trauma in Tye's life, but feeling happy that in the end everything had worked out so well. 'You were happy all round, including at your grandmother?' she remarked.

'Well, I wouldn't exactly say that.'

'You wouldn't?'

'Family skeletons,' he confided with a conspiratorial quirk to his mouth. 'Grandmother did not exactly take to Anita.'

'Ah!' Claire murmured, suspecting the fact that Anita had taken over guardianship of the senior Mrs Kershaw's charge might have had something to do with it. But, not wanting to pry into what might be a sensitive issue, particularly sensitive with the death of his grandmother so recent, Claire changed direction to ask, since Tye had just told her he had a stepbrother, 'Do you have any brothers or half-brothers? A sister per…?' She gasped, the question lost, shock taking her, her colour draining, her world spinning.

'What?' Swiftly Tye had left his seat and was standing over her. 'What is it?' He drew up a chair close to her and came and sat next to her, bending so he could see into her face.

'I'm all right,' Claire gasped, her world starting to right itself, but not so much that she wasn't glad to hang on to his forearm as quickly she asked, 'Tye—do I have a sister?'

Her eyes searched his; she needed to know. But he was taking his time answering. And it was not an answer, but a question when he replied, 'Why do you ask?'

'I think I have,' she said, and explained, 'I was about to ask you if you had a sister when suddenly I had this picture in my head of two girls—one was older, the other—I think it was me—was about five years old. We were on a beach somewhere. I'd fallen and cut my foot,' she went on shakily. 'The older girl was looking after me. Tye,' Claire said on a hoarse gasp, 'I have an old scar on my foot!'

'I noticed it,' he replied carefully. 'You had a couple of stitches in it at one time.'

She stared at him, her eyes wide. 'Do I have a sister?' she insisted. 'Do I belong to someone?' she cried.

'Oh, little sweetheart,' Tye murmured, catching hold of her hands. 'Of course you belong to someone!' And, his eyes on her pleading expression, 'You belong to me.'

CHAPTER THREE

'OH, TYE,' Claire cried helplessly. While it was an unimaginable comfort to hear him say that she belonged to him, she still desperately needed to have her question answered. 'Do I have a sister?' she pleaded. 'I need to know.'

Tye stared into her strained expression. 'I don't know,' he answered after some moments. 'I just don't know if you have a sister.'

'I never mentioned having a sister to you?' she insisted, her eyes searching his serious-eyed look.

'You never did,' he replied.

She found that odd. 'Perhaps,' she pondered slowly, her intelligence looking for an answer, 'perhaps there was some kind of family rift. Perhaps that's why I never spoke much of my family to you?'

'Could be,' he murmured, but a hint of a smile was pushing through the seriousness of his expression. 'But the good news is that your memory appears to be rousing.'

Her lovely blue eyes were huge in her pale face. 'I wish it would get a move on,' she replied, her voice barely above a whisper. And, feeling closer to tears than ever, she knew only that, despite her earlier eagerness to be out of her room, back in her room was where she wanted to be. 'I think I'll go—to bed,' she stated jerkily.

She saw him glance to her half-eaten meal, and liked him some more that he did not suggest she stay and finish it but accepted that her appetite had totally disappeared a few minutes ago. And she was so grateful to him for that, that when he said, 'Come on, then, love, let's get you back to bed,' and bent to take her in his arms, she did not resist. In any event, as Tye carried her across the hall, to her eyes the stairs looked toweringly high, and she had grave doubts that she would have managed them on her own.

They were at the door of her room when guilt smote her. Guilt that she could have been a better house guest that day than she had been. True, she and Tye were romantic partners, so from that point of view she supposed his home was her home—and that meant she was not a guest—but equally true she had been a bit less than gracious that day. In fact she had been exceedingly crabby when he had come to the bathroom door early that morning.

'I'm going to behave tomorrow,' she announced as he carried her into her room and placed her down on the bed.

Tye stared down at her. 'Don't go making rash promises,' he instructed dryly. She laughed. She enjoyed his humour. 'Want me to stay around?' he asked.

Oh, she did. Suddenly she knew that she did not want him to go. She knew that she liked him, and felt safer somehow when he was near, safer when she could see him. Then she remembered how she had kept him from his work that day, and how he had said that it was all on computer and that he could work that evening.

'Not at all,' she answered. And, feeling that was a bit blunt after his goodness, 'I'll be fine, honestly.'

Tye studied her for some seconds before accepting her answer. Then, 'Get into bed when you're ready,' he advised. 'I'll look in again before you settle down for the night.'

Claire sat in a chair for quite some while after he had gone. She thought of him, his goodness, his patience, and felt it was no wonder at all that she had fallen in love with him. The evidence that he had been in love with her was there in the ring she wore on her engagement finger. Had, however, being the operative word. Did Tye still love her?

He had never said so. Would not, in fact, have even kissed her had she not asked him to. She recalled his chaste kiss. It had hardly been a lover's kiss. Yet, who was she to complain? She was so mixed up in her head she did not know that she could cope with a stronger emotional involvement with him.

And, yet again remembering his chaste kiss, remembering how she had felt at the time, there was a part of her that seemed to want a warmer embrace from him. Uneasy with her thoughts, she abruptly got up from her chair. Too abruptly—the room spun.

Clutching hold of the bed-end to steady herself, she felt a tidal wave of frustration descend and threaten to swamp her. Instinctively she knew that she was unused to being ill and, that being so, she was finding it irksome in the extreme that she was so sapped of strength that she could not even jerk out of a chair without the risk of falling over.

She found a fresh nightdress and made her way to the bathroom, determined she was going to clean her teeth and get washed and changed without assistance.

A half-hour later she was back in bed, feeling very proud of herself and determining that, having floundered about somewhere near rock-bottom, she was now going to leave all that behind her. She was going to get better. She *was* going to recover her memory. She... There was a knock at her door. A smile came involuntarily to her mouth.

'Not asleep yet?' Tye enquired.

It was ridiculous to be so pleased to see him. She lowered her eyes. 'I've slept enough just lately to last until Christmas,' she replied.

'All part of the healing process,' he commented lightly, coming to stand by the bed and looking down at her. 'Have you all you need?'

She wished he would take a seat, perhaps stay a little while. But clearly Tye had finished his work and was minded to get to his bed. 'Yes, thank you,' she answered politely.

'You've taken your medication?'

She hadn't. 'I've decided not to take any more,' she owned.

Tye eyed her seriously. 'I see,' he remarked, and, while she sat in her bed and looked solemnly back at him, 'You've got a stubborn look about you,' he observed.

She felt stubborn, and did not want to be talked out of her decision. 'It's how I feel,' she admitted.

'Are you going to let me into your logic?' he enquired, not pressuring her at all over her decision but taking a seat on the side of her bed, seeming to have all the time in the world to sit and listen.

She began to feel bad about that. He'd had a busy day and must want to get to his bed. But, when she knew that the quickest way for him to get there would be for her to either say she did not want to talk about it or change her mind and take the wretched medication anyway, she discovered that her stubbornness would not let go.

'My head aches barely at all now.' She found she was explaining the logic of her thoughts. 'And if the other tablet is some sort of tranquilliser to stop me getting in a stew at the brick wall of nothingness I keep crashing into, then it seems to me that if I don't take that tablet I shall be much more alert to catch hold of—and keep hold of—any stray strand of a memory when it floats by.'

Stern grey eyes contemplated her at some length, then, as she looked at him, suddenly she saw his mouth begin to turn up at the corners. He stretched out a hand to take a hold of her hand, lying on top of the coverlet, and he smiled.

'What you've just said sounds perfectly reasonable to me,' he concurred. 'Though…'

His smile seemed oddly to make her spine without stiffening, and the feel of his hand holding hers was more comforting than she would ever have imagined. 'Though?' she questioned, finding she had to swallow before she could speak.

'Though it's a bit late to ring Mr Phipps and ask if he agrees with us.'

Her eyes widened and she stared at Tye in amazement.

He would ring Mr Phipps? She did not doubt that Tye had his home phone number. 'There's no need to disturb him!' she exclaimed hurriedly. 'He—'

'He *is* the expert,' Tye cut in calmly. 'The expert who, as well as being the one to prescribe your medication, has expressed the view that with a little rest and relaxation and in its own good time there is every chance your memory will come tripping back. Which leaves me wondering if, before we start running the risk of undoing all the good work he began with his excellent care and attention, should we not, out of courtesy to him if nothing else, chat it over with him first?'

Tye had asked her to let him into her logic, but something in his reasoning seemed to make her logic a non-starter. Added to which, the way he had referred to them as 'we', as if every decision made was a joint decision, seemed to weaken her. 'I...' She attempted to argue anyway, only to find that that 'we' was still getting in the way of any argument she might find.

'You're trying too hard,' Tye suggested gently, and his very tone, not forceful, but kind and understanding, weakened her further.

'You—needn't ring Mr Phipps,' she gave in.

Tye lightly squeezed her hand and let it go. Casting a glance to her bedside table, checking that she had a glass and some water, he got to his feet. 'I'll leave you to it,' he said, and was over by the door when he advised, 'Jane will be here early tomorrow.'

Claire stared at him unsmiling, but as it hit her that what he was really saying was that she must wait for her bath until Jane arrived, Claire very deliberately stuck her tongue out at him.

What was it with the man? She had expected he might be a touch offended. But, no, not a bit of it! His head went back a few degrees—and he laughed. 'Goodnight,' he said—and left her with a fast-beating heart.

She swallowed her medication and almost immediately went to sleep. But her sleep was tormented and she awoke in the early hours in a troubled frame of mind. Demons, unknown demons, seemed to be chasing her. It was still dark outside. She sat up and hurried to switch on her bedside lamp. Light illuminated the room, but a heavy sort of darkness was oppressing her.

Her breath caught in fear, but fear of what she had no idea. Tye! She thought of Tye in his room along the landing and was half out of her bed before she had a chance to think about what she was doing. 'I'll leave my door open—give me a shout if…' he had said.

From somewhere, however, she managed just then to find a stray strand of control, and got back into bed again. And as more control arrived she began to feel more than a mite ashamed of herself. Poor Tye, he had enough to contend with, trying to do his work while at the same time having to care for her while she floundered in an abyss of wanting to know so much but remembering nothing.

She left the light on while she strove to find some calm to go with that control. And a few minutes later realised she was again wondering if Tye still cared for her. He cared for her physical wellbeing, that was without question. Her mental wellbeing too, as far as he was able, given the result of her accident. But did he care for her emotionally?

That question puzzled her for quite some time. While it was true he had suggested that they keep their engagement platonic until she was fully well, she kept remembering that the only time he had kissed her was when she had asked him to. Perhaps he had gone off her? He had shown not the smallest sign of desiring her and, let's face it, to her knowledge he was used to seeing her in various stages of undress. That was to say he had seen her mainly with only her one layer of clothing: namely her flimsy nightdress, half on her shoulders half off. And once, only yesterday morning, he had seen her naked and it had made no difference. True she had bent forward to hide her breasts and the front of her, but he had sharp eyes, and she didn't doubt he had caught glimpses of her that she would prefer that he had not.

But had he desired her? Had he blazes! Not that she wanted him to, of course. But not for a moment had he shown the smallest sign of panting to, as he would have put it, have his wicked way with her.

She was starting to think that perhaps Tye might have sated any desire he had for her when they had previously been living together when she suddenly recalled how he had grinned when he had said he had given Mr Phipps his solemn undertaking that he would not make love to her—even should she beg him to.

Well, she was glad about that, even if she did feel a touch miffed that the man she was engaged to could so easily keep a lid on his emotions where she was concerned.

She fell to wondering when, if ever, she would be 'fully well'. And as she stared into a void of nothingness, so a black cloud of despair started to oppress her. Did she have a sister? And, if her mother were dead, where was her father? Surely she must have some family out there somewhere. Did nobody care about her? And who was this man lurking in that darkness, this man she seemed so afraid of that she had been totally panic-stricken when she had awakened to find Tye bending over her?

How long she stayed awake she had no idea, but eventually she found calm enough to dare to close her eyes.

In consequence of that wakeful time, she was fast asleep when Tye knocked on her bedroom door. She awakened to see him coming in carrying a tray bearing a cup of tea. She struggled to sit up.

Nothing was lost on him, however. 'Bad night?' he enquired evenly, his glance taking in the mauve shadows under her eyes.

'N...' she began to deny, but realised she was wasting her breath when Tye's glance went to the still switched-on bedside lamp, evidence in itself that she had felt the need to light part of the dark hours. But she had had enough of dark despair, so set her mind to having a happier day today, and giving Tye nothing whatsoever to be concerned about. 'I'm truly going to be on my best behaviour today,' she promised brightly.

'I don't like the sound of that. Should I start to worry?' he asked wryly.

'Not at all. You can go to work and forget I ever existed.'

'I doubt you'll be that easy to free from my thoughts. But, bearing in mind you didn't eat much of your dinner last night, are you going to eat a good breakfast today?'

She wasn't hungry. 'Er...' She was about to say she wasn't interested in food, and then realised that was hardly the way to give him nothing to be concerned about. 'I'm starving,' she lied—which fooled him not one iota.

He gave her a rueful look. 'Drink your tea and then go back to sleep,' he instructed, and left her.

In other words, Stay in bed until Jane is here. Claire obediently sipped her tea, but did not go back to sleep. She would have liked to take another shot at having a bath unaided, but could not easily forget yesterday's performance.

She was, however, feeling stronger today than yesterday, she decided, and was in the window seat watching for Jane's car on the drive when she saw her pull up at the gates, get out and open them, and then come chugging down the drive.

It was bath first, then breakfast in her room, but this was definitely the day Claire intended to stop being treated like an invalid. So, OK, there were parts of her that still ached somewhat, but enough was enough.

She had thought that Tye would make tracks for London as soon as Jane arrived. But according to Jane, who came to collect her breakfast tray and tidy around, he had been deeply involved in work in the library annexe just now when she had taken him a cup of coffee.

Claire had not thought she knew what love was, but wondered, when her heart lifted to know that Tye was still home, if it did so from the feeling of love she must have known for him before her accident, or was it just that she felt so much more secure when he was there?

She decided not to ferret at it but to just accept matters as they were. She had other things to be doing, and they did not include staying in her room all day.

That being so, but bearing in mind she was not yet up to her full strength, silently, so as not to disturb Tye, she very slowly made her way down the stairs.

She rested for a brief while at the bottom, then, being careful not to make the smallest noise, she followed her instinct and went looking for the kitchen.

She knew she was headed in the right direction when at the end of a long passageway she heard faint sounds of someone obviously busy. She opened one door—it was a breakfast room. But two doors down revealed a large and airy kitchen, and Jane.

Who stared at her in astonishment. 'Wh...?' she began.

Claire grinned. 'I thought it about time I made some sort of effort.'

'You're not fully w—' Jane halted, and changed it to, 'I was just going to make you some coffee.'

Claire rested in the kitchen while they both had coffee, and found the retired nurse very easy to get along with. Then Claire asked if she could help in any way, insisting that she needed some kind of occupational therapy.

She felt briefly happy to be busy when Jane allowed her to sit at the kitchen table and peel some potatoes for the evening meal. But that done, and no other chores in the offing, she told Jane she would like to take a walk outside.

'I'll come with you,' Jane responded instantly.

'Do you mind if I go on my own? I sort of—need to.' Claire apologised, and realised, had she not known before, that Jane must have been a special kind of caring nurse, for she understood immediately and insisted only that she must wear a coat.

Because it pleased Jane that she did so, Claire borrowed her over-large topcoat, but, for all Claire felt keen to seek new adventures, she was well aware she would not be going far. The length of the drive still seemed to be a dreadfully long walk away.

It was so good to be out, though. She breathed in the crisp October air and looked about her, marvelling that at the onset of winter the rosebeds still hosted a profusion of flowering roses.

She became quite fascinated. At home... She gave a little gasp. At home—what? She felt defeated as she recognised she had been on the brink of another memory—but it had escaped her. Feeling flattened for a moment, she felt in need of support, and went to lean against a wall of the house.

Morning sunlight warmed her, but, push though she might, the memory that had begun with 'At home...' would not come through. Her home was with Tye. Normally they lived in his London apartment. Did he have a garden there? Were there roses...? Did...? It was useless—nothing was coming through.

Her head started to ache. She moved away from the wall and, as if hoping that perhaps a closer inspection might conjure up that defiantly elusive memory, she walked over the lawn to one of the rosebeds.

She was lost for minutes as she stood looking, gently touching and bending to sample the fragrance which might perhaps kick-start that memory. But, no matter how hard she tried, the memory just would not come.

Disappointed, she turned about and was halfway to the path when she looked up. Her breath caught again, but this time in surprise. There at one of the lovely Georgian windows stood Tye. How long he had been standing there watching her she had no idea.

He opened the window. 'Like the coat!' he called.

She looked down at the all-enveloping garment. 'Well, you can't have it!' she replied smartly and, when she had never felt less like smiling, discovered as she went back into the house that she had a wide smile on her face.

Jane was preparing sandwiches and a salad for lunch when Claire entered the kitchen. 'Mr Kershaw only wanted something light, but if you'd like some soup or something on toast it would be no trouble,' Jane tempted her willingly, refusing her offer of help.

'A sandwich will be fine,' Claire replied, and, her assistance not required, she left the kitchen. She promised herself she would get back up the stairs under her own steam that afternoon, but for now she went to the drawing room.

Out of nowhere dark despair was suddenly there again, and she went to the window to stare out. Would she ever get her memory back? She tried hard to be patient, but it was not easy.

She was still staring unseeing out of the window when Jane brought her lunch in on a tray. 'You shouldn't have!' Claire protested. 'I could have come and collected that.'

'It's no bother,' Jane assured her sunnily. 'I've just taken Mr Kershaw's lunch to the library.' From that Claire realised that Tye would probably work through lunch. 'If there's nothing you need me for, I'll pop back home for an hour or two,' Jane added, tacking on that she would return to see to dinner and anything else, and departing.

Claire waved to her when she went by the drawing room window, but had not moved when the sound of the drawing room door opening made her turn round. Tye stood there, tall, grey-eyed and friendly.

'What have I done to you that you prefer to eat your lunch alone?' he asked, his glance taking in her untouched lunch tray.

'I thought you'd be working.'

His answer was to come and take up her tray. 'I'll show you the library,' he offered.

She went with him purely because she was pleased to see him.

The library was larger than she had imagined, lined wall to wall, its shelves almost up to the high ceiling, with books ancient and new. 'Wow!' she exclaimed. 'You said library, but this is something else.'

'My grandfather was something of a collector,' Tye replied, and, placing her tray down on a round, highly polished antique table, he showed her the next-door room. It was the room he had called the library annexe but which now, with its computer, laptop and about every other piece of modern technology, looked more the last word in an up-to-date office than anything.

His own meal tray was on a side table, and he collected it and placed it beside hers on the table in the library. He drew out a chair, inviting her to take a seat. When she was seated he took a chair next to her and selected a sandwich.

'So, given that I'm fairly certain you descended those stairs without help, and probably have plans to make a solo return, how's the best behaviour plan going?' he enquired.

She enjoyed his light humour; he had the ability to temporarily lift her feelings of desolation. Then she remembered her other solo trip, that one over to the rosebed, and she urgently asked, 'Do we have roses at your—our—other address? Our home in London?'

'You've remembered something?' he asked, his look alert.

She shook her head. 'I was on the brink... Out by the roses... There was something there, but it had gone before I could catch it.' She sighed, finding it terribly difficult to be bright. 'I really, really think I should stop taking those tablets,' she said a degree mulishly.

'You're assuming they are tranquillisers. They may not be,' he hinted. 'How's the head?'

She had a thundering headache if he really must know. She helped herself to a sandwich she had no particular interest in, took a neat bite without tasting it, and told him, 'Jane makes a fantastic sandwich.'

Claire glanced at him then, and saw a sensitive kind of look in his eyes. 'You'll get there,' he promised quietly.

She stared into those sensitive eyes, and found she was blurting out that which had occupied many of her thoughts. 'Do you still care for me, Tye?' Feeling herself going a trifle pink, she looked from him. 'I mean, I know you are caring for me, none better, but—can you still love me?' She wished, heartily wished, when an age passed without him answering, that she had not said anything. 'I'm sorry,' she mumbled. 'I've embarrassed you.'

'No, you haven't,' he denied, and to prove it he placed an arm about her shoulders, gave her a brief hug. A light-humoured note was back in his voice when he said, 'And as for loving you, my dear—who could fail to love you?' He took his arm away. 'Now, eat your sandwich!' he ordered bossily—and she laughed.

All in all, Claire reflected, as she lay in her bed that night, given that her headache had seen her having to resort to taking her medication, it had been rather a splendid day. True, she had endured many a dark moment in pursuit of that reluctant memory, but she had made the stairs, up and down, on her own—twice. She had, as common sense, her headache and instructions from Tye had decreed, returned to her room to lie down for an hour or so during the afternoon, but by evening her headache had cleared and she had joined Tye downstairs for dinner.

Tye had been a superb dinner companion, conversing on all and everything save her accident, her family and her lack of memory. He had been so thoughtful too—deliberately, she realised, never once referring to any of the things they had done together. She owned she would not have minded if he had perhaps tried to remind her of some outing or other they had shared. It might well have triggered some memory or other. But today had been Best Behaviour Day, and, since he was so interesting to listen to, she'd been on her best behaviour to go along with anything he decided upon.

He had walked back up the stairs with her, in no hurry when, while going as fast as she could, she realised it must have been torturously slow for him.

Claire settled down to sleep, recalling how they had said goodnight at her door and she had gone into her room, washed and changed into her night things—and had taken her prescribed medication. Sleep put an end to her pleasant reverie.

She awakened with a start about four hours later when the gremlins of the previous pre-dawn morning returned to storm in and assault her. She awoke afraid and troubled, and almost knocked over her bedside lamp in her anxiety to find the light switch.

She was awake for a long, long while as she did battle to control the nightmare in her head. As a result, she awoke again at eight to find a cup of tea going cold by her bedside, indicating that Tye had already been into her room.

He returned again shortly before nine and her heart seemed to somersault in her body. He was immaculately suited, good-looking and sophisticated with it, and was clearly not intending to stay home that day. For a moment she panicked. She did not want him to go.

'Was it something I did?' she asked.

He looked indulgently down at her. 'I'll hang on for Jane, then I'll be off.'

'Will you be home tonight?' she asked, pushing anxious fingers through her tousled blonde hair, try as she might, unable to keep the stress she felt out of her voice. Tye was her anchor—she would be floating about in a sea of nothingness without him.

'I may be late, but I'll be back,' he promised, and she immediately felt guilty again.

'You don't have to,' she assured him quickly, starting to

feel dreadful. 'I don't want you rushing back here if your business is more than you can complete in one day!'

'And what if I *want* to come back here?' he asked indulgently.

'Am I being a pain?'

'Considering what has happened to you, I think you're being very brave,' he answered seriously. And, while she did not think she was being very brave at all, 'You've nothing to worry about,' he assured her. 'Jane won't leave you on your own.'

Claire felt a shade awkward that Jane was going to have to give up her day to keep her company, and she wanted to tell Tye that she would be all right on her own. But her experience of those early-morning gremlins had badly rocked her.

'Well, have a lovely day,' she said brightly. She smiled cheerfully up at him, and thought for one nebulous moment that Tye was going to bend down and kiss her.

Her heart did a crazy flutter at the infinitesimal movement he made towards her, only for it to steady when he seemed to check, then smiled. 'Be good,' he bade her, and strode from her room.

She stayed staring after him for some time, knowing then, if she had not known before, that he was fully aware of her feelings of insecurity. She supposed that feelings of insecurity were probably all part and parcel of starting a new life—as of a few weeks ago when she had awakened in hospital with absolutely no memory of her past or of who she was. Perhaps it was all part of that insecurity that she did not relish the idea of being in the house by herself, of being alone for hours on end, when that dreadful despairing feeling of hitting that brick wall of nothingness would assault her again.

She watched from the window as Tye drove away in his car. And wanted him back with her. But he had work to go to, and she was being selfish, and he thought her brave—and she wished that she were.

When Jane came upstairs to be near while she had her bath, Claire determined that she was going to be truly brave from now on.

So that when just after lunch Jane let slip that she had not walked her neighbour's dog that day, Claire, renewing her 'truly brave from now on' determination, suggested, 'If you want to take him for a walk now, I'll be fine on my own.'

'Oh, I couldn't possibly,' Jane responded.

'Of course you could,' Claire countered with a smile, but did not find it easy to persuade Jane. Eventually, however, with Jane insisting she take down her mobile phone number just in case she wanted company, Jane drove off.

Left on her own for the first time, Claire tried to keep her mind clear of gremlins and concentrated her thoughts on anything but her need to know all and everything that had been wiped from her mind. Black despair was forever hovering, but it had been easier to cope with somehow when someone else was in the room.

She said her name out loud. 'Claire Farley.' She did not feel like Claire Farley, but then, for that matter, she did not feel like anyone else either.

She was in the drawing room when the phone rang. It made her jump. She was alone. There was no one else there to answer it. What if it was a business call for Tye? She realised she had no choice but to take the call.

'Hello?' she said.

'What sort of a day are you having?' It was Tye's voice. Her heart lifted.

Please come home. 'Quiet, relaxing and restful.' She told him that which she thought he would like to hear. How wonderful of him to ring!

'You're getting on all right with Jane?'

'Absolutely,' she replied, and suddenly realised that he

had probably only rung to speak to Jane anyway. 'Did you want to have a word with her?' she asked, finding she had hit another blank spot when she tried to think up some excuse for Jane not being there.

'I rang to speak with you,' he answered pleasantly, which pleased her on two counts: she wasn't going to have to lie—no way was she going to tell him Jane was not there—and Tye had rung to speak to her.

'Did you want anything in particular?'

There was a pause, but she was sure there was a smile in his voice when he did answer. 'Can't a man ring to speak to his platonic fiancée without an inquest?'

She could not keep from smiling. 'I'm glad you did. Ring, I mean.'

'Good,' he replied. 'You're behaving yourself again today?'

'My behaviour is impeccable,' she answered.

She realised the phone call was over when he stated, 'I'll see you some time tonight.'

She did not want him to go. 'Bye,' she said. It seemed a pride thing that she said it first.

'Bye,' he replied. She thought he added, 'my darling,' but guessed she must have misheard. He had, after all, not a minute ago reminded her that their engagement was, for the time being, a platonic affair, and a softly spoken 'my darling' just didn't fit in with that.

She stayed in the drawing room reflecting how extremely glad she felt that Tye had taken the time out of his busy day to ring to say hello. Then she suddenly became aware that she was playing with the ring on her engagement finger. It felt comfortable there, as if it belonged there. She smiled.

By the time night had fallen, however, her smile had long departed. Dark clouds were descending. She knew that she was not doing herself the least bit of good by pushing and pushing for some kind of memory of her past, but she just did not seem able to stop. She needed to know—and there was nothing there.

Out of courtesy to Jane, who had decided not to stay the night but would not leave until Tye came home, Claire tried to hide the despair she felt. When, though, shortly after an early dinner, Jane reminded her that she was still in a state of convalescence and added that this was the longest she had been out of bed without a rest, Claire was grateful for the suggestion that she had an early night.

In her room, she wondered what time Tye would be home. Again she found her fingers on her engagement ring. He had said he would return home that night, but she felt so agitated suddenly that she wanted him home now. Somehow everything seemed better when he was there.

Another hour ticked by, and her feeling of agitation had grown and started to mingle with feelings of utter despair. Knowing she just could not stay alone in her room another minute longer, she was about to leave her bed to go downstairs to find Jane when all at once she heard the sound of a car. Tye was home!

Instantly, just knowing he was near, she began to feel less fraught. She wanted to see him, but started to wonder if, after his long day, he would come in to see her. Jane would tell him that the day had gone without mishap, so he would have no need to come and check on her.

Claire heard the sound of Jane's car starting up, and knew she was making tracks for her own home. Claire felt so grateful to her. She did not know how she would have got through the day without Jane. While it was certain that Tye without doubt was rewarding Jane handsomely, it all the same had been an awfully long day for Jane.

Claire made up her mind she would be more in control in future. The next time Tye had an early-morning start she would insist that there was absolutely no need for her to have someone with her. Although with nothing in her head but blankness she had to face that she might never recover her memory! She tried not to panic at that thought, but knew that she could not go through the rest of her life with some-one for ever in attendance.

Claire decided then, since no matter how hard or how desperately she pushed and prodded for some kind of mem-ory—for any kind of memory—with nothing coming through, that she was straight away going to be more pos-itive than she had been. Then there was a light tap on her door—and Tye appeared.

A smile instantly beamed to her face. 'I didn't think you would pop in!' she exclaimed, her relief, her pleasure evident.

'And what sort of a fiancé would that make me?' he asked lightly, coming over to the bed and looking down at her. 'How did your day go?'

'I wanted to ask *you* that!'

'The day went well,' he replied, paused for a moment, and then added, 'Jane tells me she left you on your own for a short time while she took her neighbour's dog for a walk.'

'I insisted. But I wasn't going to tell you.'

'We can't have secrets.'

'I don't know *any*!' Claire responded frustratedly. But immediately apologised. 'I'm sorry. After your long day you don't need me to get all stroppy.' She smiled at him and confided, 'I've decided that from now on I'm going to be more positive. More—'

'You're doing very well as you are,' Tye cut in firmly, reminding her, 'It's barely a month since you went sailing through the air. Both your body and your head need time to mend. You mustn't rush these things.' She supposed she must have looked a little bleak, for, as though believing he had been a little severe in his lecture, Tye smiled encour-agingly. 'Sleep now,' he said, and bade her goodnight.

'So, I'll be positive,' she determined when he had gone, and, ignoring the demons that had a tendency to wait until dark to come and trounce her, she bravely switched off her bedside lamp. She instantly wanted to switch it on again—but would not.

Eventually she fell asleep, but only for that sleep to be again tormented by demons—giant, faceless demons. She choked on a sob and woke up—woke up in absolute terror. Her mouth was dry, her breathing laboured, and she was far too panic-stricken to remember how she was going to be more positive in future.

In that awful darkness the thought that she might never recover her memory was just more than she could take.

Groping frantically for the light switch, she sat up. Light flooded the room—but by then she was in such a ferment it was of little help. She did not seem able to think straight. What was she doing there? Who was she? Where were her family?

Tye should know. But Tye did not seem to know—not very much anyway. Once more she found herself on a merry-go-round of pushing and pushing at the night-black shutters of nothingness. Her head ached, throbbed. Despite her medication her head felt as though it was splitting in two. She seemed to sense that there was a memory—some memory—that was near—yet she just could not pull it through that dense mass of pitch blackness.

Along with her panic came fear. She felt lost and alone. Felt too as if her head was going to explode as she tried desperately to break through that dark solitude of emptiness. Tried until she was totally both mentally and physically exhausted. And still nothing would come.

She attempted to lie down, to calm down, but the moment she closed her eyes, even with the light on, a crushing weight of dark wretchedness closed in on her. She jerked upright, scared and so alone. Frightened, but of what she knew not.

Terror gnawed at her, chased her, and all she knew then was that she could not take any more of this blank, black nothingness. Without further thought she shot out of bed.

She needed Tye. Everything was all right when he was there.

Tye had said he would leave his bedroom door open. She felt so in need of having someone to hold on to then that, as she flew to her bedroom door, she knew that if his bedroom door was not open she was prepared to open every door on that landing until she found him.

But that proved unnecessary. In the light streaming behind her from her own room she could see that a door two doors down was ajar. Claire was not thinking but was acting solely on instinct when she hurtled into that room, crying out *'Tye!'* as she went.

Afterwards she supposed that he must be the kind of man who slept with half an ear on the listen, for even as she rocketed into his room he was sitting up in bed and putting on the light.

'Tye!' She cried his name again, and went flying over to him. She guessed her face must be showing her agony of mind because as, heedless of the strain she was placing on her healing muscles, she dashed to him, so he opened his arms and gathered her to him.

'It's all right. You're all right. I'm here,' he soothed, his arms round her, holding her to him, stroking her hair. 'Bad dream?'

'I think I'm going mad,' she whispered fearfully.

'No, you're not,' he comforted her. 'You're safe. You're doing fine,' he encouraged.

But her terrors were not so easily forgotten. 'Can I sleep with you?' she asked, her voice a thread of shaken sound.

'I…' He seemed to hesitate—until he looked into her ashen and afraid face. Assessing the situation in that one look, he hesitated no longer. 'Climb aboard,' he invited gently, and as he pulled back the covers so she should get in, so he eased himself away and to the edge of the bed. 'Close your eyes while I get something on,' he instructed, and only then did she notice what she had been too traumatised to notice before—that she had been comforted against his bare chest.

He was gone only for a few seconds and, as his broad chest was still bare, she vaguely gathered that he must sleep naked and had left his bed merely to don a pair of undershorts.

'Come here,' he said softly, joining her under the covers. Without hesitation she moved to him, and he took her into the secure haven of his arms. Gently then he eased her to lie down, tucking her head into his shoulder and tenderly stroking the side of her face. 'Try to sleep,' he suggested softly.

A dry kind of sob left her. 'I'm sorry,' she apologised.

'Poor lamb,' he breathed.

'There were demons and gremlins and...and...' She couldn't go on; she was shaking.

'I've got you now. Try to relax,' he murmured.

'You won't make me go?' She supposed she meant back to her room.

'I won't make you go,' he promised. 'Just lie quietly. I'm here.'

'You won't put the light out?' she begged on an urgent whisper.

'I won't.'

'Hold me. You'll hold me?'

'I'll hold you, little love,' he gave his word.

'And you won't let me go?'

'I'll never let you go,' he promised.

CHAPTER FOUR

SHE stirred in her sleep. She felt warm, safe and secure. More secure than she could ever remember. That feeling was not to last! She drowsily moved her legs—and met other legs! Her eyes flew open. She saw that the bedside lamp had been left on, but took more heed of the great strident alarm bells that were suddenly clamouring—she was not in bed alone!

Hard-muscled strong male arms were around her, holding her close! She swallowed hard, and then it was that she knew why she felt so snug and warm: her back was against a naked male chest, and all at once his skin was burning through the thin material of her nightdress. With everything within her in one tumultuous uproar, she on that instant jerked out of the man's hold.

He was at once awake, and as she, her body protesting at such rapid movement, leapt from the bed, so he, immediately alert and watching her, was getting out of bed his side and reaching for his robe.

'Who are you?' she exclaimed, shock making her voice throaty. She knew then that up until a month ago she had never lain eyes on the man.

'You don't remember?' he questioned, his tone quiet, his eyes concerned. He looked as though he would come over to her, but did not.

'My head's alive with memories!' she exclaimed.

'Your memory has returned?' he asked, and again appeared about to come to her to comfort and reassure her, but again stayed where he was. 'You don't remember me?'

'I do. Yes, I do,' she answered.

She started to come out of her shock and looked at him—

his short robe revealing so much of his all-masculine legs, part of his broad chest showing through the opening of the garment. But that was when she became overwhelmingly aware of what she must look like standing there facing him. Suddenly she was horrifyingly conscious that the expensive nightdress she wore was next door to transparent.

Burning colour surged to her face and she swiftly brought her arms in front of her. 'Oh!' she cried in anguish, but was spared further embarrassment when Tye, awake to her action, glanced to her crimson face and took charge.

'Go back to your room,' he instructed calmly. 'You remember where it is?' he asked, a frown creasing his forehead as though he was considering that with the return of her past memory she might have lost more recent memory. She nodded, important other matters starting to crowd in. 'Go and get into bed. I'll join you—that is, I'll come and see you—in a very few minutes.'

She did not waste a second. She wanted to see him. Questions were going off like fireworks in her head, shooting in all directions. But just then it seemed important that she get some clothes on. With her head reeling, she went quickly—perhaps too quickly.

Whatever, on reaching her room she found that with her head being bombarded, memories flashing in and flashing out, being overridden by other memories, by sad thoughts, she had no mind or energy to look for fresh clothes. In any case, she now knew that she never dressed without showering first.

That thought lightened her mood. That thought triggered off the wonderful realisation that, yes, she definitely had her memory back.

Her emotions began to be mixed. While she was starting to feel exhilarated that she could recall such a small thing as showering every morning, she also began to fear that her memory might swiftly go again. She was striving hard not to panic at that thought when she heard Tye coming along the landing.

Conscious again of her flimsy covering, and with no time now to get dressed, she hastily got into bed—just as her fiancé came into the room. Fiancé? Her memory was a blank on that one. She stared solemnly at him when, now clad in shirt and trousers, the tall man came over to the bed and stood looking down at her.

'What's my name?' he asked her, his expression equally solemn.

'Tye,' she answered huskily. 'Tyerus Kershaw at my service.'

His mouth quirked upward at that. 'You've awakened with a sense of humour,' he remarked softly, remembering as she obviously did that that was how he had introduced himself to her at Roselands clinic. 'And what's your name?' he probed.

She had no trouble with that one. 'Larch Burton,' she told him.

'Your memory is returning?'

'Most of it, I think. Who's Claire Farley?' The question seemed inconsequential as soon as she had asked it.

'You were in Farley Ward, and someone thought Claire suited you,' Tye answered, and went on with what she supposed must be relevant to him from his point of view. 'You remember the accident?'

She tried hard to think, but had no recollection whatsoever of any accident. She shook her head, and, feeling a touch panicky, 'Will my memory go again?' she asked urgently.

'I shouldn't think so,' he replied straight away. 'But, until he can get here, Mr Phipps wants you to rest quietly.'

'You've been in touch with Mr Phipps?' she exclaimed, amazed.

'He's on his way.'

'From London?' she gasped, feeling utterly astonished.

'He lives about ten miles away.'

'You must have got him from his bed!'

'He's a doctor—he's used to it.' Tye smiled at her. 'I'll get you a drink of something…'

She didn't want that. 'Don't go!' she cried, adding rather desperately, 'In case I lose my memory again, I live in a village called Warren End; it's near High Wycombe in Buckinghamshire.'

'You don't live in London?' Tye asked, coming to take a seat on the side of her bed.

She shook her head, moving her legs to give him extra room. 'That's where I was when the accident happened, wasn't it?'

He nodded. 'Do you remember why you were in London?'

'I…' That was a question she did not want to answer. It brought back memories of a kind she did not want to remember. 'No,' she said stubbornly.

If Tye suspected there was more to it than that he gave no sign, but changed tack to question, as though the question was more important, 'Are you married? Some married women prefer to not wear a wedding ring.'

'Not married,' she answered, which prompted the memory that she was wearing this man's engagement ring. 'Why—?' she began, but he was cutting in with another of his important questions.

'Do you live with some man? Have you any special manfriend?'

'I live with my sister—and her husband,' she mumbled. 'Why am I wearing your engagement ring? We can't be engaged or you wouldn't have had to ask me about other men in my life.'

'My, you have woken up sharp,' Tye commented lightly, but said seriously, 'I shouldn't be questioning you like this. Shall we leave it until after Miles has seen you?'

'Miles?' she queried, questions in respect of their engagement sent temporarily to the back of her mind.

'Miles Phipps,' Tye answered. 'My stepbrother.'

'Mr Phipps is…?' Larch guessed that this was her day for surprises. 'Why—?'

'You're going to get me into serious trouble,' Tye broke in. 'I'm supposed to be keeping you calm.' He smiled encouragingly. 'We'll talk later. But for now you should be resting while we wait for Miles to arrive.'

From where she was viewing it, Larch could not see any reason why Tye should have called his stepbrother to chase over to Shipton Ash to see her. 'But…' she started to protest, but anything further she might have asked died in her throat at Tye's stern look.

'Do you trust me?' he asked bluntly.

She did not like his tone. 'How could I not?' she exclaimed belligerently. 'I've just spent half a night in your bed—to no avail!'

He laughed, and she found she loved his laugh. It immediately sent away her sudden sour mood. 'You'd have died on the spot had I tried anything,' he taunted, and reminded her, 'You know full well that I gave my word to Miles that I wouldn't lay a sexual finger on you.'

Larch realised she had gone a shade pink, but discovered she was not one to back down in a hurry. 'Always the bridesmaid!' she sighed, but smiled. 'All of which makes you rather a nice person.'

'Oh, to wear such rose-tinted spectacles,' he said. 'How are you feeling now?'

'More in control than I was, but still excited that my memory—or most of it—seems to have come back.' A look of pleasure appeared on her face. 'I *do* have a sister. Her name is Hazel, and she is a lovely person, and—'

'And nothing,' Tye cut in. 'Either you're going to keep quiet and rest, or I'm going to have to leave you.'

Larch stared at him, her heart starting to flutter a little.

'I'll be good,' she promised. 'Only there are so many questions…'

'I know,' he agreed, but got to his feet saying, 'Perhaps it would be a courtesy, considering I've roused Miles from his bed, if I went and opened the gates for him. You'll be all right?'

'Of course,' she answered, but the moment he had gone found she could not sit still in bed. She found her wrap and went to sit in the window seat.

From there she saw Tye emerge and head up the drive. It was only just starting to get light, and as Tye approached the iron gates, so she saw car headlights appear. Tye opened the gates and got into the passenger seat. Never one to waste time, she guessed he was filling his stepbrother in as they drove down to the house.

She returned to bed, hoping with all her heart that Tye left out that bit where she had fled from her room in the middle of the night and had hurled herself into bed with him. Had she *really* done that? In the cold light of day it seemed incredible that she had done any such thing.

She was sitting up in bed, the covers up to her chin, when Tye brought his stepbrother into the room. 'I hear you don't care for the name we gave you,' was Miles Phipps's cheerful greeting.

'I'll put some coffee on,' Tye stated, and tactfully left them.

In all, Miles Phipps was with her for around twenty minutes, but Larch rather thought he had seen, heard and taken in all that he needed to in the first five minutes of his visit.

He was an exceedingly clever man and spent the rest of his visit in what might have appeared to be casual chat but from which, from her responses, she realised, he was probably able to confirm his assessment.

She realised too that he was more Miles Phipps, stepbrother to Tye, that morning, than Mr Phipps, eminent consultant, when he put away his bedside manner, suggested she call him Miles, and asked how she found life at Grove House.

'I've been extremely well looked after,' she replied.

'You're looking far better than you did,' he observed. 'When Tye proposed that you should come here, I thought the tranquillity and peace might aid your recovery,' he revealed.

'It's lovely here,' she agreed.

'You know that I would not have sanctioned you coming with Tye were I not aware that he is a man of the most unimpeachable integrity?'

'I know he is.' She smiled, and hoped she did not look as pink as she felt as she recalled how she had gone to his room and asked if she could sleep with him. The only finger he had lain on her had been in a touch of comfort.

Miles Phipps got ready to leave. 'Any missing pieces of memory will most likely filter back during the next few days,' he advised. 'And when the first rush of adrenalin at knowing you are back to being Larch Burton again begins to fade, it's possible you may start to feel a little low. I don't foresee any major problems,' he assured her. 'Though I'd still like to check on you again—say, in about a month's time. Meanwhile, if you have any worries, please don't hesitate to contact me.'

She thanked him so much, and felt quite a fraud when he had gone that Tye had roused him from his bed on her account. But she supposed she must still be feeling a little euphoric in that her thoughts were almost immediately chasing away, hither and thither.

Guessing that Tye would not see his stepbrother on his way without the coffee he had spoken of, Larch decided she had time to take a quick shower and get dressed. She felt much stronger now than she had felt even two short days ago, but was not yet ready to risk taking another bath without Jane being around.

Larch was collecting fresh underwear together when it suddenly struck her that no wonder all of her clothes looked new. They *were* new! Had never been worn. Oh, heavens! She had assumed, accepted, that because Tye had said they lived together he had packed only her newest things that day he had brought her case into the clinic. But he had not only brought them, he had *bought* them—paid for them. Purchased them because she had never lived with him, and the only clothes she'd had were those she had been wearing and which had been cut from her at the hospital!

Larch was in the shower when the low point Miles Phipps had spoken of came, sooner than she had expected. Suddenly it hit her that, since she had not lived in London with Tye, since she was absolutely nothing to him, and in fact must have been a total stranger to him, she had no right at all to be here at Grove House!

She had no idea what the engagement ring on her finger was all about, but what she did know was that she had no business to be here, accepting his hospitality. It was at once plain to her then that soon—today, obviously—she was going to have to leave.

She did not want to go. She wanted to stay here with Tye. She… Abruptly she blanked that thought and hurriedly stepped from the shower.

She was drying her left foot when she noticed that neat scar again. A smile came to her serious mouth. She knew what that scar was all about now. Her smile faded as she recalled her parents. Long before her mother's illness their parents had taken her and Hazel for a seaside holiday. That holiday had included a hospital visit when Larch had cut her foot on some broken glass some careless person had left lying about on the beach. Hazel had been upset and had half carried her back to their parents.

Larch was in her room, dressed and ready to face what had to be faced, when Tye tapped on her door and came in. As he must have observed she was showered and dressed, so Larch saw that he must have showered too, for he was now clean-shaven.

'I thought you might have been up to mischief,' he commented dryly on her decision not to wait for bathtime aid. 'I've made some fresh coffee. Would you like it here or downstairs?'

They obviously had to talk. Just as she obviously had to return his ring to him. 'Downstairs,' she opted, but found she had used up quite a lot of physical steam, and that when it came to going down the stairs she had little energy to hurry.

Tye did not offer to carry her, and for that she was grateful. He kept slow pace with her, enquiring as they went, 'Things settling down a little?'

'I'm getting over the initial shock, and so thankful to have my memory back,' she replied.

Tye escorted her to the drawing room and left her briefly while he collected coffee from the kitchen. When he returned he waited until she was seated on a sofa, a low table in front of her, before he handed her a cup of coffee and took a chair on the other side of the table.

'I—um—I'll leave, of course,' Larch found she was blurting out. 'It's very kind…'

'Leave?' Tye seemed most surprised, and placed his coffee cup and saucer down on the table. 'Oh, I don't know that I can allow that,' he informed her nicely.

'You can't allow?' Perhaps because she did not want to go, Larch had to push herself to aggressiveness. 'You can't stop me!'

She stared belligerently into steady grey eyes that clearly stated that stop her he would, if he wanted to. But when she was fully expecting a load of hostility from him—and she would hardly blame him after the way he had taken her in and seen to her every need—he calmly picked up his coffee again. 'I know this can't have been the most pleasant few days of your life,' he remarked, 'but I truly don't think you are physically fit enough yet to go anywhere.' Stubbornly she would not answer, and he went on, 'Has it really been so awful for you here?'

She immediately capitulated. 'Oh, Tye, you know it's not you or your lovely home. Just as you know I've had some dreadful dark moments here, you must know how well I've been looked after. And I appreciate that, I really do. It's just that I have no right to be here. No right to disrupt your household, to disrupt your work, to—' She broke off and found she was staring down at her left hand, staring at the wonderful engagement ring. Feeling for some odd reason the utmost reluctance, she slowly drew the ring from her finger. 'I have no idea why I've been wearing this, but I know now that I have absolutely no right to wear it.' She stretched a hand out and placed the ring down on the table between them. Her engagement finger felt lost without it. 'There are still a few gaps in my memory, but we never were engaged, were we?'

Tye was quiet for a few seconds before, making no move to pick up the ring, he replied, 'No, we never were.'

'And I'm positive I would have remembered had we ever lived together,' she went on, and, her face suddenly flaming, 'I can't believe that I actually came to your room last night and asked if I could sleep with you,' she gabbled in an embarrassed rush.

'Don't think about it. You were having a torrid time in that unrelenting dark void,' Tye said, and he smiled as he tacked on, 'I was fully aware that you had no designs on my person.' She gave a sigh—he had such a devastating smile.

Swiftly she bucked her ideas up. 'I'm getting away from the point; there's so much going on in my head,' she explained, 'I don't know which bit to tackle first.'

'Let me help,' he offered, and she immediately began to feel selfish.

'You've done more than enough for me,' she replied.

'I've interrupted your work for long enough. You must be wanting to get to your office and...'

'I'm not going to London today.'

'You're not?'

'Not.' That teasing expression she knew so well came to his face. 'You've forgotten,' he accused. 'We were going to tackle a walk outside today.' Oh, Tye. Just then she could not think of one tiny reason why she would want to leave. 'But let's get some priorities sorted here. The hospital contacted the police with your description in case anyone should report you missing—your details will have been circulated. So far no one has come forward looking for you. But now you've remembered you lived with your sister and her husband, perhaps we should phone them to let them know you're safe.' His expression suggested that he did not know why they should bother if her sister could not stir herself to report her missing. But he had referred to getting priorities dealt with first.

'Hazel has been away for some weeks...' Larch paused to do a few simple calculations '...but she's due back home—er—tonight, I think. She's on an extensive working-while-training study course in Denmark. Hazel's an accountant with a firm of auditors who are expanding over there,' Larch explained. She was proud of her sister who, with a natural aptitude and through sheer hard work, was doing so well in her career.

'Your sister furthers her European knowledge at weekends too?' Tye enquired.

Larch wasn't sure that she did not resent his inference that Hazel either stayed in Denmark at weekends or cared not, when she returned to spend weekends at home in England, that Larch was not there.

'Hazel rang—' Larch broke off, nausea taking her as she remembered.

'What's wrong?'

'Nothing,' she quickly denied, and could only suppose

that her feelings of revulsion had shown in her face. Hurriedly she got herself together, and explained, 'Hazel rang—it must have been the day I went to London.' Larch knew full well it had been that day—that fateful day of her accident. She hadn't spoken to Hazel—Neville had. 'Hazel rang to say she had a seminar to attend the next day, Saturday, and also had an endless backlog of studying to catch up on. She wanted to know if we would mind if she didn't come home that weekend.' Neville had minded—my stars, how he'd minded! He had tried to take his frustration out on her. 'Anyhow,' Larch continued, trying to wipe the terrible scene that had followed from her mind, 'Hazel must have decided to stay on in Denmark until all her work and studying is complete. But...' Suddenly it dawned on Larch that if Hazel *had* been home in the last month then there must be some very special reason why she had not reported her missing. 'W-would you mind if I rang home—just in case Hazel's there?'

Without a word Tye went and brought the telephone over to her. Larch's home number came readily to her and she dialled, hoping that Hazel was not there. She could not bear the thought that her dear sister might have spent the best part of a month going hairless with worry about her. If Hazel was not already home, then, Larch thought, just in case her sister arrived home first today, she would leave a message on the answer-phone to say she herself would be home at some time that day.

The ringing out tone stopped. But, to Larch's disquiet, it was not Hazel who answered the phone but Neville, Hazel's husband. Larch overcame her aversion to speaking to the man to enquire, 'Is Hazel there?'

'Well, well,' Neville sneered, evidently recognising her voice, 'if it isn't my errant employee.' And, his tone changing, 'Don't bother coming back—you're fired!' he said nastily.

As if she would want to work for him again! Though,

while wanting to thank him for that good news, Larch had more important things on her mind. 'Will you give Hazel a message for me?'

'If I ever see her again! She seems to have taken root in Denmark. All in the good name of advancement!' he added spitefully.

'Hazel hasn't been home since—?'

'Not since you decamped to go and stay with your mother's godmother, leaving me and my office high and dry in the process!'

She was not interested in his office; he exploited his staff mercilessly, and, given she was not at all sure how she could explain to Hazel why she had left her job, Larch was very pleased she did not have to go back to work for him.

'She's phoned, though?'

'Once! And then only to ask for Ellen Styles's phone number—apparently your godmother is ex-directory. What a pity I couldn't find my wife's address book,' he said sarcastically, causing Larch to know he had not bothered to look for it. 'I take it Hazel hasn't managed to phone you?'

Larch had known that matters between Hazel and her husband were going through a bad phase, but it sounded as though they had deteriorated dramatically. Hazel had thought him wonderful once, and probably, beneath their present disharmony, still did.

'Would you give Hazel a message if she gets home before me today...?' Larch began.

'Tell her yourself! She's not coming home until Tuesday!' Neville Dawson retorted, and slammed down the phone—and Larch started to panic. That was until Tye's voice broke in on her thoughts, causing her to have to fight to get herself more of one piece.

'Your sister's not home?' he enquired evenly.

'She's not coming back until Tuesday,' Larch said without thinking.

'You lived in your sister's home with them, I think you said?'

Larch had not actually said that, but the fact that half the house belonged to her, she and Hazel having inherited it jointly from their parents, was hardly an issue, Larch felt. 'Just the three of us,' she agreed, but got herself together to tell Tye, 'I must have told Neville—Hazel's husband—that I was going to stay with my mother's godmother for a while. There are a few blank spaces in my memory,' she explained, wishing she could forget Neville Dawson's assault on her and never, ever remember it again. 'But the fact that my accident happened in London seems to suggest I was on my way to spend some time with my honorary aunt Ellen.' Larch had no memory at all of catching a train to London. But another memory flashed in. 'Aunt Ellen insisted at my mother's funeral that I go and stay with her whenever things got too much for me.'

'Your mother *is* dead?' Tye probed gently.

'Both my parents,' Larch answered.

'Oh, my dear,' Tye murmured, and, as if he could not help it, he came to the sofa where she was and, taking hold of her hands, sat down beside her. 'How old are you?' he asked, as though thinking she was young to have suffered such a loss.

'Twenty-three,' she replied, but felt weepy suddenly and needed to not think of her parents just then. 'As Aunt Ellen obviously hasn't been in touch with Neville, I can only suppose I either intended to ring her when I got to London or rang her and she wasn't in—it's all a blank,' she ended lamely. 'I remember leaving my house, and—'

'And now you're offending me by suggesting you want to leave mine,' Tye got in smartly.

'Offending…' She was appalled. 'Tye, I don't want to offend you! You must know that I don't!' she exclaimed swiftly. 'But you're not responsible for me—nobody is, for that matter. But—'

'Tell me,' Tye cut in, 'does your sister's husband work?'

Larch had no idea what tack Tye was on now, but saw no reason not to answer. 'Yes, he does.'

'From home?'

'No, he has an office. I don't know what he was doing at home today. Perhaps he forgot something and went home for it. He has a manufacturing company in…'

'So if I took you home today you'd be in the house by yourself during the day, with no one there to look after you?'

'I…' Oh, heavens! It only then dawned on her that, with Hazel in Denmark until Tuesday, there would be no one else in the house but her and her ghastly brother-in-law. She felt sick at just the thought, and wasn't sure she had not lost some of her colour, but felt honour-bound to point out, 'N-Neville doesn't normally work at the weekends. He'll probably be there tomorrow and Sunday.'

'But not for the rest of today or Monday and Tuesday?' Tye paused, then said, 'It's not on, is it, Larch? Truly now,' he pressed when she did not answer. 'Look at you,' he went on. 'You're looking drained now. Are you going to undo all Miles's good work? The work of the nurses, not forgetting Jane, who have all worked hard to make you well again? There will be no one at your home to make you so much as a cup of tea.'

While Larch was perfectly certain she was quite able to make a cup of tea for herself, she was just as certain that Neville would let her starve before he thought of making a meal. 'I'll be fine,' she protested.

'You're intent on going?'

Without Hazel there, Larch had the greatest aversion to entering again that house she had run from in such panic. The only alternative was to go and stay with Aunt Ellen—which, Larch felt, suddenly feeling as drained as Tye had suggested she looked, was hardly fair. To go and park her convalescing self on the frail elderly lady… 'I can't impose on your hospitality any longer,' Larch stated stubbornly.

'So, for the sake of your obstinate pride you'd go?'

'But—why would you want me to stay? Until a month ago you'd never set eyes on me. We are not engaged—I have no hold on you.'

'Yes, you have!' he retorted.

Her heart was suddenly thundering. 'I have?' she asked faintly.

He bent to pick up the engagement ring, his expression hidden, and she watched while he slipped the ring into his pocket. Then he looked at her and said, 'I've grown to like you, to like having you here,' going on logically, 'You have no one at your home, while here you have Jane, and you have me.' His handsome mouth picked up at the corners. 'And my grandmother would have loved you to stay.'

Larch smiled at that, and could feel herself weakening. It wasn't right to impose on his hospitality, and she knew that it was not. But Tye had said that he liked her and that he liked having her there at Grove House. Bleakly she thought of the alternative: going back to spend the weekend alone in the same house as her odious brother-in-law. Oh, she couldn't. She just couldn't!

Solemnly she looked into the steady grey eyes that were silently watching her. 'Say you will?' he urged gently.

She opened her mouth to tell him no. 'Tye…' She hesitated—and found she was asking, 'M-may I stay until Tuesday?'

He smiled that devastating smile. 'I'll make us some breakfast,' he said.

According to Tye, she needed time and space in which to adjust to having recovered her memory. With that in mind, after breakfast he suggested that she return to the drawing room and rest on a sofa for a while.

Whether these instructions came from him or from his stepbrother, she had no idea, but while it was true that her head was abuzz, she felt she had rested more than enough. She was about to say as much when it came to her that Tye probably had work in the library annexe that he would not mind getting on with.

'You want to go and get on with some work, don't you?' she asked.

He looked as though he would deny any such suggestion. But, as if reading her mind, 'I can spend time with you if you prefer,' he replied.

That did it. 'I'll be in the drawing room if you need me,' she stated—and loved it when he laughed.

Tye occupied quite a lot of her thoughts that morning. At other times, though, she was remembering happy times, sad times, and times that she would far rather forget. She supposed it was only natural that that last encounter with her awful brother-in-law should be the most dominant memory.

Up until the age of fifteen, her childhood had been little short of idyllic. Then her mother had fallen ill—the prognosis had shattered their world. Within a year her mother had been confined to a wheelchair. By that time Hazel had been doing extremely well in her career and, while it had been unthinkable that their mother be looked after by strangers, it had been equally unthinkable, for all Hazel had tried to insist, that she give up her career to take care of their mother and their home.

The obvious solution had been for Larch to take over. 'You'll have your chance later,' her distracted father had promised when at sixteen Larch had willingly left school. She had not wanted to think about later—her mother had been given two years' life expectancy.

As it happened, her mother had lived for another seven years. Larch wondered if she would have died then had not their father been involved in an accident that had killed him.

Having expected that their mother would die first, it had been a tremendous shock when nine months ago they had attended their father's funeral. A month later, their mother had given up her struggle.

Larch was bereft. So too was Hazel. Hazel no longer lived at home, having met and married Neville Dawson. But Hazel had come home to stay with Larch for a few days after their mother's funeral and, more business-minded than Larch, had taken on the task of looking into the family's financial affairs.

It was Hazel who had found their father's will and sorted out any complications involved in him leaving everything to their mother, but in the event that she predeceased him everything was to be split equally between their two daughters.

As Larch had known in advance, Hazel was scrupulously honest and fair, insisting that she read everything and understood everything. What Larch had not known until Hazel confessed was that Neville Dawson's business was in trouble and that it needed a cash injection.

'Neville's suggested that we sell this place,' Hazel had gone on. 'But, apart from the fact I wouldn't dream of foisting such a decision on you at this present time, it's going to take an age for Mum and Dad's estate to be sorted out. Which means we won't be able to sell anyway. What I have suggested, having looked at it from all angles, is that Neville and I sell our apartment and—only if you're agreeable, of course—we move in with you. What do you think?'

'I'd love it!' Larch jumped at the suggestion. She felt terribly adrift without her parents, and was hurting inside from losing them. To have Hazel home would be a joy. Larch had had very little to do with Neville, so did not know him too well. She assumed, because Hazel was such a very nice person, that he would be very nice too. Wrong!

Their apartment was in a much sought-after area, and it sold quickly. Hazel, perhaps realising how bereft her younger sister felt, arranged to move in straight away. Then she turned her attention on to Larch personally. 'When the estate is settled you'll have enough money to enable you to train for a career of some sort. Is there anything in particular you would like to do?' she asked.

Although having done very well in her school exams seven years ago, all Larch's recent experience had been in attending her mother and home-making. 'I'm sure I'd like to do something, but Mum and Dad—' She broke off to get her feelings in check. 'It was so sudden—I can't seem to think about the future.'

And that was when Hazel told her that Neville was always looking for office staff, and how did she feel about doing a temporary stint in one of his offices to see if an office atmosphere suited her?

Larch was willing to try anything, and at once started work. She quickly absorbed the job content, but in no time she was discovering first-hand why Neville Dawson had such a high turnover of staff. The man was a slave-driver!

At first she was glad to be busy. Busy enough to be able to push sad thoughts of her parents to the back of her mind for short spaces of time. But she was not sleeping well. There was no respite at work, and when the person who had given her work instructions one day exploded at the pressure and walked out—and was not replaced—Larch found she was doing the work of two people.

She began to feel stressed, and wanted to leave the company, but around that time Hazel came home with the exciting news that she had been singled out for huge advancement, which included a three-month stint working, training and studying in Denmark. By then Larch had become aware that her sister's marriage was not all the sweetness and light she had allowed them to believe that it was. Larch had no wish to be a cause of further friction between husband and wife by leaving his company. And by then she was certain, knowing more of her sister's husband, that he would go on and endlessly on about the chance he had given her and look at the thanks he had received. Larch kept quiet and her temporary job became permanent.

Then, in the week that Hazel flew to Denmark, another member of staff walked out, and more work was piled on to Larch. She could not cope. She started taking work home. She worked late and slept little, and began to feel utterly worn out. She did not know for how much longer she could take it.

Matters came to a head a couple of weeks later. It was that Friday she raced out of her home, heading, she rather thought, for Aunt Ellen's home in London. That whole week had been particularly stressful for Larch. And on Friday there had been no let-up. She had taken work home, knowing that Neville Dawson was very much anti the Burton sisters for some reason, but she was feeling glad that Hazel would be arriving home for the weekend later that night.

Larch made Neville the meal he was expecting and then shut herself away in her bedroom. She had only just started on the work she had brought home to complete when she thought she heard the telephone ringing. She was half off her seat when, knowing that Neville would answer it, she sat back down again. The way he had begun to look at her sometimes was starting to make her skin crawl, and she did not wish to have more contact with him than she had to.

Then suddenly her bedroom door was violently thrust open. She jumped out of her chair in surprise, and was horrified when Neville charged in, his eyes bulging as he spewed out the result of Hazel's telephone call. Furiously he mouthed out why Hazel was not coming home that weekend—and weren't they lucky they probably wouldn't see her again until she had finished her work in Denmark? And wasn't *he* lucky too that he had been the one to answer the phone? It had not been him her sister had wanted to speak to but *her*!

With each word he grew more and more incensed, and Larch began to feel alarmed at the expression on his face when he came closer and closer, belching out his tirade. But she began to feel quite terrified when, threateningly near, he caught a hold of her by her shoulders and began mouthing words that indicated if he could not have Hazel her sister would make an ideal substitute. With that he yanked her up against him, his mouth clamping on hers making her want to heave, his weight forcing her on to her bed.

Three times she scrabbled off the bed, and three times he forced her back again. Furiously she fought him and some-how—she had no recollection of how—she got free of him on her fourth attempt. She had no memory of picking up her shoulder bag, but since it had been with her at the accident she knew that she must have. What she did remember was her flight down the stairs, the rattle of the front door as she slammed it behind her. She recalled falling over in her haste to get away, recalled barely stopping to get up but racing as she got to her feet, and then running, running, running… And then—nothing until she had woken up in a London hospital.

A shudder went through her, and so engulfed was she in that terrible memory of Neville Dawson attempting to force himself on her that she had no idea that the drawing room door had been quietly opened. Not until, 'My dear!' Tye exclaimed, 'What is it?' and came quickly over to her.

Her breath caught, and she could only imagine that the horror of that memory must have shown in her face. 'Nothing,' she at once disclaimed. Aside from loyalty to Hazel, Larch felt totally incapable of sharing that memory with anyone.

Tye was not prepared to be put off, it seemed, as he probed, 'You remembered something very dreadful?'

'Not all memories are happy memories,' she answered obstinately, and, having had enough of being cosseted, even if she wasn't back to her full fitness by some way yet, 'If you're very good I'll make you a sandwich for lunch,' she offered.

From his lofty height he studied her. But when she had a distinct feeling that Tye was not the sort to veer from finding out that which he wanted to know, possibly because he was judging that this day might be proving stressful enough for her, he did not press her to tell him the very dreadful matter she had remembered.

'Jane's coming in to fix dinner and a snack lunch. If *you're* very good we'll take a walk up the drive.'

Larch was on her feet in no time, and went from the drawing room and into the hall with him to see that he had been upstairs to collect a heavy sweater.

'It's cold out,' he said, handing the bulky sweater to her from the newel post.

'For me?'

'You'll look stunning,' he promised, and grinned, and her heart seemed to tilt. 'Hang on to my arm,' Tye instructed as they left the house and went by the rosebeds.

She found she had a contrary streak and did not want to hang on to his arm. Was it contrary, though, or was she suddenly shy of hanging on to him? Grief, woman—you've *slept* with the man!

'At home, my father used to love his roses,' she said in a rush, then took a calming breath and put her hand through the crook of Tye's arm. Funnily enough, she found it felt comfortable there.

'How long ago did you lose him?' Tye asked.

'Nine months ago—ten months ago now, it would be,' she replied, realising her hospitalisation had taken care of one month. It seemed to her then that perhaps it was about time that she opened up a little about herself. Tye, after all, need not have taken her in and looked after her so splendidly. She could not bear to think how she would have coped had she been left to her own devices on her discharge from the hospital, where she would have gone, how she would have fared. 'My mother was terminally ill,' Larch volunteered. 'W-we never expected to lose my father first.'

'Your mother died recently?'

'A month after my father.'

Tye's hand came to her hand in a touch of sympathy. 'You lived with your parents?'

She nodded, feeling a little choked, but overcame the moment to tell him, 'It was a pretty ghastly time afterwards, so Hazel suggested I did a temporary job in her husband's company while I made up my mind what I wanted to train for. A bit old to start training, I know.'

Tye quickly sorted through what she had so far said. 'You'd previously stayed home to care for your mother?' he asked.

'I treasure that time of being with her,' she answered quietly, then coughed on a husky throat and charged, 'You didn't know I was working for my brother-in-law when you told me I was "between jobs" when I asked you?'

He neatly ignored the charge. 'You're not going back to your temporary job.' It seemed more of a statement than a question.

'No,' she answered.

'Have you decided what you want to train for?' he asked, halting just short of the gates at the end of the drive.

'Not yet. But I have discovered I'm pretty quick with figures, so perhaps I'll follow Hazel into accountancy. I'm quite nifty on the computer too, by the way,' she informed him, her eyes twinkling.

He looked down at her, and perhaps recalled how two days ago she had asked if she had much computer experience. 'This is far enough for today,' he decided, turning about. 'How are you feeling?'

'Wonderful!' she replied, and smiled a sunny smile.

They returned to the house and the question that had been burning on her tongue was there again—how had that engagement ring got onto her finger? But she was suddenly again conscious of what Tye had done for her, and in consequence how very much she had intruded on his work. And she became afraid of intruding further.

'Thank you for the loan of the sweater,' she thanked him politely.

'Hang on to it; you might want to slip out from time to time,' he suggested.

'See you later,' she said nicely, not wanting to delay him any longer. Though she was conscious of him standing watching her as she headed for the drawing room.

When Jane arrived and learned that Larch had her memory back, it transpired that, because of the possibility of her memory returning when Tye was not there, he had briefed Jane on the exact position of their relationship.

'This is great!' Jane beamed, and could not help but give Larch an impulsive hug even as she warned, 'Now, you mustn't go getting over-excited. You still need to take things easy.'

Having been used to being busy, it was starting to get to Larch that she had done nothing for ages. A sure sign, she realised, that she was improving by the hour. But she had bigger concerns than her present enforced idleness. Apart from having to tell Hazel that she was not going to go back to working for her husband, how was she going to tell Hazel that she wanted to move out and get a place of her own?

The idea of having to return to her lovely home where Neville Dawson now lived was nauseating to her. She did not want to do it. With Hazel getting on so well in her job, being promoted to the more expanding European side of the business, there was every likelihood of her frequently working away from home.

The thought of staying in her home alone with Neville Dawson was something Larch could just not take. Yet, since he was her sister's husband, and Hazel loved him, there was absolutely no way she could tell Hazel of his assault on her.

Tye worked through his lunch and Larch had a snack with Jane in the kitchen. Jane allowed her to help with the dishwashing afterwards, but, taking a close look at her, suggested, 'If you're hoping to stay down for dinner tonight, it might be an idea to take a rest this afternoon.' Larch thought it about time she ceased her redundant lifestyle, but before she could offer to help out a little Jane was going on, 'Mrs Lewis from the village is coming up to do a spot of cleaning,' and Larch realised that she might be in the way.

'I'll see to my room,' she told Jane, and went upstairs, her head again filled with flashing past memories of her life at home.

Then all at once, as she sat in what was now her favourite window seat, she found she was remembering snatches of her life after she had run, terrified, away from her home. Remembering—and questioning.

Clearly now she could remember Tye sitting quietly by her in the hospital, quietly watching and quietly talking to her. She remembered how quietly vigilant he had been. And yet—he didn't even know her!

Why, when she was a stranger to him, had he said that they lived together at his London home? Larch puzzled over that for some minutes, before suddenly realising that Tye had never actually said that they lived together. It had been she who had said, 'We live together, don't we?' Oh, grief, she remembered now. She had followed that up with, 'Do I sleep with you?' Oh, the poor man—he must have been embarrassed to death!

Larch stayed in her room physically resting, but with her head chasing one thought after another. She had lost her memory in an accident and had assumed Tye must have heard of the accident and come looking for her. But it hadn't been like that, because Tye hadn't even known her then. So how, if she hadn't been able to tell them, had they found her fiancé?

They had taken it as gospel that Tye was her fiancé—so how had that come about? She had no idea. What she did know, however, was that when she had run in fear from her home that Friday she had not been wearing an engagement ring. Yet when she had awakened to the world in hospital, some time later, there was definitely a ring on her finger.

It was time, she rather thought, that she started to ask a few pertinent questions.

CHAPTER FIVE

LARCH felt she would never be out of Tye's debt when, early that evening, she donned a white shirt and black trousers that he had purchased for her.

'Did you go and buy these personally for me?' she asked Tye when she joined him in the drawing room.

'Of course,' he answered briefly, but was more interested in how she was than in any fashion statement she might be making. 'You were supposed to rest this afternoon,' he accused, as though to suggest that she had not.

'I did!' she protested. 'Physically, anyway. My brain's been dormant for so long it's no wonder it has some catching up to do.'

'You haven't remembered anything to upset you?'

'Not at all!' she answered smartly—perhaps too smartly. Tye did not appear convinced.

'As you know, Miles mentioned the cause of your amnesia might not be solely on account of your accident.'

'Oh?' she answered, just as if she did *not* know.

'There was a possibility you were suffering some trauma you were trying to blot out,' Tye persisted. She did not want to lie to him but how could she tell him how distraught she had been, not only on her own account, but that her brother-in-law should have betrayed her dear sister in such a despicable way? 'Losing your parents the way you have is a tragedy on its own, Larch,' Tye pressed when she made no answer. 'Did something else traumatic happen to you that you needed to blot out?'

'I—er—told you I was good at figures. I found I was doing the work of two people. I suppose it could have become more than I could cope with. It worried me.'

'Your brother-in-law took advantage of your family loyalty?'

You could say that. 'I honestly don't want to discuss it,' Larch replied dejectedly. 'That makes me sound mean, after your goodness to me, but—'

'Forget it!' Tye cut in. 'I'm attempting to aid your recovery, not make you unhappy. Let's go and eat.'

Larch went with him to the dining room. She took her place at the table, feeling fairly certain that Tye—whom she knew had not forgotten the way she had yelled at him when she had woken up to find him bending over her—was aware that there was some happening in her recent past that she wanted to keep dead and buried.

How could she tell him? It sounded so—tacky. Again she thought of the way she had gone and got into bed with Tye. Heavens above, what a difference in two men! Tye so trustworthy. Neville so awful—and her poor sister was married to him. She couldn't go back home to live; she couldn't— she just could not.

'Don't dwell on it, Larch!' Tye sharply interrupted her thoughts. Proof enough, should proof be needed, that he knew that it was not just pressure of work that had pushed her to that welcoming vacuum of memory loss.

'This suet pie is delicious,' she answered, and smiled.

'Jane will have us both as fat as otters,' Tye replied, his mouth quirking nicely upwards.

'Are otters fat?'

'I've no idea,' he answered, and Larch just burst out laughing.

'And they said the Hatter was mad!'

Tye's eyes were on her laughter-lit mouth. 'So, tell me about the men in your life?' he suggested.

'Men?' Her laughter had gone.

'Boyfriends.'

She relaxed. 'Who had time for boyfriends? I was working every—' She stopped suddenly, realising she had an opening here that she did not intend to waste. 'And anyhow, what would I be doing with a boyfriend when…?' She left the question there and changed tack to ask, her expression serious, 'How did I come to be wearing your engagement ring, Tye?' It was only then, though, that it came to her that he could not have purchased the ring especially for her. 'I'm sorry,' she immediately apologised as she guessed that the ring had probably been previously worn by his ex-fiancée. 'If it's painful…'

Tye leaned back in his chair, his eyes on her sensitive face. 'I suppose it's inevitably painful when someone you care for dies.'

Her breath caught. 'Oh, Tye,' she replied huskily. 'Your fiancée died?'

He shook his head. 'I was never engaged.'

Larch studied him solemnly. 'So how did I come to be wearing that ring? Where did it come from if—?'

'Let me explain,' Tye cut in, and began, 'I lived here at Grove House for quite some while as a child, and stayed here often in my growing years. I was a more frequent visitor when my grandmother became frail and housebound. But even in her frailty my grandmother was staunchly anti her two daughters-in-law—my father's first and second wives,' he inserted. 'That being so, when my grandmother died and I realised that at some time someone was going to have to personally go through her belongings, I knew I'd have to be the one to do it.'

'You couldn't possibly ask one of them to do it. Your grandmother would have hated that.'

'How well you understand,' he said, but went on, 'I did think of asking Paulette, my stepsister-in-law, but somehow that didn't seem right either. Anyhow, one has certain duties, and…'

'You're far more sensitive than you want anyone to know,' Larch interrupted gently.

'Shut up,' he replied, but the quirk at the corners of his

mouth took any sting from his words. 'I came across the ring in my grandmother's bedside drawer. It was her engagement ring—I knew I would never have need of it.'

'You think it unlikely that you'll ever marry?'

He looked from her to cut into his meal, then gave a shrug as he replied, 'Highly unlikely, I'd have said. I haven't reached thirty-six without having a few—encounters...' She'd like to bet that 'a few' was an understatement... 'but I have never felt so much enamoured that I'd want to ask any woman to be my wife.' He swerved from that particular subject to go on, 'Bearing in mind my grandmother's antipathy for her daughters-in-law, it wouldn't have felt right to have passed the ring on to one of them. I decided that Paulette might like to have it.'

'Miles Phipps's wife?'

Tye nodded. 'I didn't have time then to drive from here over to Miles's place, so I slipped the ring into my pocket with the idea of stopping by the hospital where he mainly works and handing it over for him to have it enlarged for Paulette. My grandmother had incredibly slender, delicate fingers,' he explained. 'With both Miles and I so busy, it's easier to meet in London than elsewhere.'

'You went to the hospital where I was first taken?'

'That's right. I knew from experience that any appointed time I make to see Miles stands a fair chance of not happening because of some emergency or other, so I went to the hospital when I thought he was about to come off duty.' Tye glanced across at her. 'He *was* held up—you were the emergency that came in before we'd had the chance to more than greet each other.'

'You were there, at the hospital, when I was brought in?'

'Poor love, you were out cold.'

'Oh,' she murmured, and thought he looked a touch disquieted as he remembered. Ridiculous! She pulled herself together. 'So...?'

'So, with Miles obviously busy, I made myself scarce and decided I could just as well see Miles the next day.'

'You came to the hospital again the next day?'

'And again Miles was busy with a patient. I decided to save myself another journey and wait a short while to see if he would be free. While I was hanging around I saw the nurse who'd been with you the previous evening and asked after the young lady who'd been brought in. She said where you were, and that they'd probably let me see you if I went up to Intensive Care.' He shrugged. 'It didn't look as if I'd be seeing Miles for ten minutes or so…'

'So you came to see me?'

'You were still unconscious—in a coma.'

'You came again, after that occasion, to see me?'

'It seemed mean not to. Everybody else in that hospital was having hordes of visitors. Poor Larch—or Claire, as you were shortly to be—there was no one visiting you.'

'It was very kind of you to bother.' She thanked him.

'I told you, I'd led a selfish life.' He grinned. 'My grandmother was prodding me in the back.'

'Did she also prod you to put that engagement ring on my finger?' Larch asked with a smile.

'Ah, that,' Tye replied. 'A new nurse, one I hadn't seen before, had just come on duty that day. You were still in a coma, with no sign of coming out of it. I was sitting beside you, looking at you and hoping that you would soon wake up, when I happened to glance at your delicate hands. It was then that I realised I had only ever seen such beautifully long narrow fingers once before. My grandmother's.'

'Really?' Larch queried, taking a look at fingers she had never given any great thought to.

'Don't ask me why—perhaps for something to do—there wasn't a lot going on—and I still hadn't managed to pass the ring over to Miles, though I'd still got it with me—before I knew it I'd taken it from my pocket and tried it on your engagement finger. To be honest, I was staring at it, slightly incredulous at what I'd done, when it dawned on me that the ring was a perfect fit.'

Larch smiled, picturing the scene. 'Did I get to go to the ball?'

'You got to make me more amazed when, after lying there lifeless for a couple of days, perhaps because of the unaccustomed feel of the ring around your finger, you suddenly started to show signs of life.'

'How? Wh…?'

'There am I, feeling slightly foolish, I admit, when you do no more than curl your hand into a dainty loose ball.'

'I alarmed you?'

'Not at all. It was the first sign that you might be waking from your unconscious state. I got the nurse over to you fast. The next time I paid you a visit you'd been moved to a different part of the hospital.'

'Was I awake then?'

'You were in a kind of twilight world for a short while,' he replied. 'No bones broken but a body that was in pain and in need of healing.'

She supposed that 'twilight world' was about right. She had probably been sedated into the bargain. 'Why didn't you take your ring back?' she asked. 'There must have been an opportunity.'

'There was,' he agreed. 'Only by then the ward you'd been transferred to was guarded by fierce dragons. Said dragons transformed into little angels when one of them, aware of your engagement ring, took me for your fiancé. After that I was allowed to visit you without restriction.'

'Why would you want to? Visit me, I mean? You didn't know—'

He shrugged, and cut in, 'I passed the hospital most every day—it wasn't such a great effort.' His mouth quirked. 'Besides, you'd got my ring.'

She felt her lips tweak too. 'You could have taken it any time.'

'Like I said, while you were still being carefully monitored, as your fiancé, I got to see you whenever I cared to.'

She wanted to ask him why he would care to, but that would make it seem as if he really did have a personal interest in her, and she suddenly felt shy to presume so much. 'You let me think I was engaged to you,' she recalled. 'I can remember asking you if I was engaged to you, and you…'

'I let you believe that you were.'

Her heart hurried up its beat. 'Why?' she just had to ask.

'You'd only recently come to an awareness that you had no memory. You were scared, understandably so. You were alone, vulnerable. You needed something solid, some constant in your life.'

She clearly remembered her feelings of panic. That lost and alone feeling. He was so right. 'That was kind of you,' she murmured. Was it any wonder that she was in love with him? She stifled a gasp as the suddenness of that knowledge struck, and pulled herself sharply together. She would be drooling over him any minute now, and he must not know. 'But—why…? I mean…' She struggled to find the right words. 'That constant, yes, I needed that, and I do so thank you for it. But to extend your kindness, to put yourself out to the extent that you brought me here to Grove House. Fed and clothed me!' Suddenly she was feeling overwhelmingly discomfited.

'You're blushing, you're feeling awkward, and there's absolutely no need,' Tye stated sternly.

'Apart from anything else I've intruded on your personal life!' she blurted out, feeling hotter than ever.

'No, you haven't. I hadn't, nor do I have, anything in any way pressing in my personal life. Besides which, while I haven't yet fully decided what I want to do with Grove House, by being here we're able to keep the place aired and lived in.'

'I'll go home tomorrow,' she stated, as in all fairness she

felt that she must. Oh, my word—his expression was suddenly as black as thunder.

'We've been through all this!' Tye rapped sharply, clearly a man who did not care to repeat himself. 'There's no one at your home to look after you. And if you think I'm going to allow you to undo all the good work that has been done in getting you this far in your recovery, then...' He gave her a harsh look, and she didn't like it at all.

'Then I can think again?'

'Exactly!' he said heavily.

And she did not want him angry with her—she found it too upsetting. 'Are you going to give me a hand with the dishes?'

She thought his lips twitched at her swift change of subject. 'Jane will...'

'I'm not leaving these for Jane to do in the morning,' Larch told him decisively. He might have got his own way in that she would not be asking him to drive her to her Buckinghamshire home tomorrow, but by no chance was she going to leave a pile of dirty dishes in the sink when she went to bed that night.

As things turned out, while Larch did not ask Tye to drive her anywhere the next day, drive with him she did. It was his suggestion when he asked, 'Coming for a drive?' that the stimulus of seeing something other than the inside of the house would do her good.

She wanted to jump at the idea, but love and a feeling that she had already encroached too much on his time made her hold back. 'You don't have to...' was as far as she got.

'Would I if I didn't want to?' he questioned, and, throwing in a killer, 'Am I not entitled to see something other than the four walls of an office either?'

'Oh, well, if you put it like that. Can I borrow your sweater?'

He laughed, and she loved him all over again, and, having kept his sweater, went to her room to collect it. She had no idea of when she had fallen in love with Tye. It was just there.

It was a joy being out with him. Sometimes they chatted; sometimes they didn't. Proof that she wasn't yet back to being her old self was there, though, in the fact that on two occasions she found her eyes were closing and she was drifting off into a light sleep.

They had lunch out and arrived back at the house around three that afternoon, having motored all around—but nowhere near Buckinghamshire. 'I really, really enjoyed that.' Larch thanked him.

'So did I,' he answered, and, with her eyes shining, she found it incredible that such a simple statement could make her feel so happy. She went to her room to rest, as he had instructed. Though more from her point of view so he should have his own space.

Larch felt she had progressed physically in leaps and bounds that weekend. She felt so much better than she had, and in fact barely ached at all. And only then, thinking of how she had been, did she fully appreciate the punishment her body had taken.

Her headaches were almost a thing of the past too, and it was so good to have her memory back, for all her thoughts seemed to begin mainly from the time she had become acquainted with Tye. He seemed to be the centre of her universe. She understood now, of course, why he had never referred to any of the things they had done together, why he had not referred to her family. The simple reason being that, until he had come across her in hospital, they had never *done* anything together, had never been anywhere together. They had, in fact, been perfect strangers to each other.

When Larch was not thinking of Tye, her thoughts went to her sister. Which inevitably brought to her mind that vile memory of Hazel's husband.

Larch wished she could confide in Hazel as she had always done in the past. But this was one occasion when the last person she could confide in was Hazel. It would destroy her to know what the man she loved had attempted.

Now, more than ever, did Larch *not* want to return to her old home. But where else was there for her to go? Initially, anyhow. She would have to move out, but what on earth was she going to tell Hazel?

Larch was up early when Tuesday morning came around. She could not settle to try to go to sleep again. With her head spinning, having tried half the night to think up some way to tell her beloved sister that day that she was leaving the home they owned, Larch left her room and made her way down to the kitchen.

She set the kettle to boil, knowing it was impossible for her to stay in the house she had been born and brought up in. Yet what could she say that would be acceptable to Hazel? The truth would crucify her! But to stay, not knowing how soon or how often Hazel might go away again, leaving her alone in the house with that man, was more than Larch could contemplate.

She poured boiling water into the teapot with her spirits somewhere down around her feet. She would dearly love to see Hazel again, but oh, how she did not want to leave Grove House—and Tye.

It started to worry Larch that since Tye knew she would be returning to her home that day he might offer to drive her. Her stomach heaved at the thought that she might arrive before Hazel. Neville might be there; she might be alone in the house with him!

'You're up and...' At the sound of Tye's voice Larch spun round. So deep in her thoughts, in her revulsion, had she been that she hadn't heard him come in. But Tye was staring at her. 'You're ashen!' he exclaimed, and coming over to her he caught hold of her arm and guided her to a chair. 'Did I scare you?' he asked, taking a chair next to her, his eyes searching her face.

'It's not you,' she answered chokily, totally without thinking.

'Who, then?' he questioned, and appeared determined to have an answer. She shook her head—how could she tell him? But this time it seemed he was not prepared to let her get away with it. '*Some* man scared you, though, didn't he?' he pressed.

'Don't…' she whispered. 'Tye, don't.'

Gently he took her hands in his. 'I think it's too late for "don't", wouldn't you agree?'

She tried to deny it, but with his grey eyes steady on hers she found it difficult. 'It—it isn't only me,' she replied at last, only vaguely aware that she was in her night attire, while Tye appeared to be wearing a short robe and nothing else.

'This man who attacked you—he attacked somebody else?' Tye insisted.

'No!' she exclaimed. 'It was just me…' Her voice trailed off. 'How did you…? I didn't say I'd been attacked!'

'You didn't have to! Something has had a very profound effect on you. It caused you to be terrified that night I came to check on you and you woke up unable to immediately recognise me.'

'It's all right,' Larch told him hurriedly, hoping he would accept that and leave it there. No chance!

'Whatever happened is still haunting you, Larch,' Tye said quietly. 'And I would be failing in my care of you if—'

'Oh, Tye,' she butted in unhappily. 'Your care of me has been excellent. But I cannot allow you to—'

'You cannot stop me,' he cut in pleasantly. 'Now, as I see it, we have three options.'

'No, we don't.'

'One,' he went on, as if she had not spoken, 'we get outside help—I can ring Miles and ask him which professional body would be the best for you to see.'

'I don't want—'

'Two, you can tell me what happened to you that has you drifting off into unpleasant thoughts too frequently since you regained your memory four days ago.'

'Do I do that? Drift off?'

'You do. Quite plainly something is tormenting you. Three…' He paused, then, looking deeply into her lovely blue eyes, 'Or three, I shall have to tell your sister my suspicions and…'

'*You can't!*' Larch exploded. 'You *can't* tell Hazel!' she repeated feverishly, rocketing off her chair, too panic-stricken suddenly to be able to sit still.

But Tye was on his feet too, reaching for her, drawing her to him in a hold of comfort. 'Shh…' He quieted her, his left arm holding her close, his right hand gently stroking her blonde hair.

Oddly, when she had been feeling so alarmed, after about a minute of being gently held by him Larch began to feel calmer. 'It's so—tacky,' she whispered into his shoulder.

'Who was it?' Tye asked quietly against her ear. She could not tell him. 'Someone you knew?' She swallowed and clutched on to his arm. 'Your—sister's husband?' Tye, perhaps recalling she had told him she hadn't time to have boyfriends, made another guess. Larch's gasp of breath told him that his guess was accurate.

She pulled out of his hold and went back to the chair she had rocketed from. 'Perhaps it was my fault,' she suggested disconsolately.

'A classic victim reaction!' Tye stated sharply, resuming his seat and bending towards her. 'Trust me, Larch, whatever happened, I know that you are completely blameless.'

Any sharpness in his tone was negated for Larch by *his* absolute trust in *her*. 'What I meant was that, had I not been so both emotionally exhausted from Hazel and I losing our parents and mentally worn out from trying to keep on top of my workload, I might have had something left over to be able to deal better with the situation when…' She did not want to think about it, but in all honesty wondered if she could have handled it better had she not been so tired when confronted by the lecherous madman Neville Dawson had become. But, remembering how it had been, she suddenly knew that there was nothing she could have done to change anything.

'Situation?' Tye probed, not allowing her to go away from him.

'Hazel phoned—that Friday,' Larch began. Tye had guessed anyway. And tacky, sordid, as it was, she now saw little point in holding it in any longer. Nor, now that she knew of her love for Tye and knew implicitly that she could confide in him, did it seem as disloyal to Hazel as it once would have. So Larch went on. 'She wanted to speak to me, so Neville said. He was furious about it. Anyhow, I was upstairs in my bedroom, doing some office paperwork, when—when he burst in and—and...' Her voice faded away until she became aware that Tye had taken a hold of her hands again in a hold that seemed to give her courage, and she felt more able to continue. 'Anyhow, Hazel had rung to say she wouldn't be home that weekend, and Neville was in a rage. He came crashing into my room without knocking, grabbed me...' It was all so vividly there as she relived it, all so real that she could hardly breathe, but she made herself go on. 'He forced me onto the bed...' Her voice dried, and as her face started to crumple, 'I was t-terrified,' she cried, her voice fracturing.

'Oh, my dear,' Tye mourned, holding her hands tightly, and there was something in his voice that seemed so much as if he was suffering as much as she was suffering that Larch found the strength to try and make things better.

'I eventually managed to somehow get free—before he could carry out his intention,' she said in a rush. 'I don't remember stopping for anything. I just shot out of the house. I must have grabbed up my bag as I went. I had it with me anyway in hospital—when, although I didn't appreciate it then, I mercifully couldn't remember anything.'

If she had not known before of Tye's wonderful sensitivity, she knew it then when he tenderly raised one of her hands to his lips and placed a most beautiful healing kiss on the back of it.

And quietly he documented, 'Aided by that traffic accident, your exhausted physical, mental and emotional self was shut down by nature until you were rested enough to cope again.' He gave the hands he held a small shake, and then asked, 'You feel better able to cope now?'

'Oh, yes,' she answered, and with more confidence than she felt. 'Naturally I shall move out from there as soon as I can.'

'You intend to leave your brother-in-law's house?' Tye enquired, sounding as though he thoroughly approved of the idea.

'It was never his house,' Larch answered. 'Our parents left it to Hazel and me.'

'That man has no right there?'

'Well, he is my sister's husband,' Larch pointed out. 'Anyhow, as soon as I can think up some sound reason to give Hazel for wanting to move out, I'll go.'

'You don't intend to tell her the truth?' Tye questioned sharply.

'Good heavens, no! I *know* that the man she married is not worthy of her, but Hazel doesn't know it. Sometimes they're a bit scratchy with each other, but she loves him very much. It would destroy her if she heard so much as a whisper of what he is capable of.'

Tye was silent for some long moments, and then commented, 'I don't think you're as strong yet as you like to believe you are.' Adding, 'It could be quite some while, Larch, before you're fit enough to live on your own.'

The same thought had occurred to her. 'I'm getting stronger, day by day,' she answered with a smile.

'And what will you do, while still living with your sister, should your brother-in-law come after you again?' Tye wanted to know.

She wished he had not asked—that same horrendous thought was something else that had plagued her. 'I'll be all right while Hazel's there.'

'And when she isn't?' He was starting to sound a shade difficult. 'What about when she's at her place of work, or in Denmark again, or when her husband returns home during the day—as he did last Friday?' Tye reminded her, unnecessarily, as if determined to bring all her fears out into the open and deal with them.

'I'll be able… And anyway, I'm sure he won't try anything like that again,' she answered, wondering which one of them she was trying to convince. Then, changing the subject completely, 'Would you like a cup of tea?' she asked brightly, getting up and going over to the teapot.

Tye came and stood by her as she poured out two cups. Astonishingly he had let her get away with her non-answer. And she realised that he must be accepting that soon she would no longer be his responsibility—not that she ever had been.

Though let her get away with it he had, as she handed him his cup and saucer so blue eyes met grey, and all at once she was not at all certain about the hard glint that had suddenly appeared in his eyes. It worried her.

'I—er—think I'll take my tea back to bed,' she said, and as quickly as she could she went from the kitchen and back up to her room.

When Larch next went down the stairs it was to find that Jane had just arrived, as had the cleaning lady she had spoken of.

Jane introduced Mrs Lewis, who had worked at Grove House before and was familiar with the lay of the house, and as she went off to start work Larch hid her feelings behind a smile as her spirits took an instant dive. If Jane was here there was every chance that Tye would shortly be leaving for his London office. Perhaps he had already left! Perhaps he would not be home until late tonight.

Larch held down a knot of raw emotion at the thought that she might never see him again. She knew her sister well enough to know that Hazel would not hesitate to come and collect her the instant she knew that she had been in hospital.

'I've a dental appointment this afternoon,' Jane was explaining as she busied herself about the kitchen. 'I thought I'd make a casserole for this evening. All it will need then will be for either you or Mr Kershaw to switch the oven on to heat it through.' Larch felt too dispirited to mention that she would not be there that evening to partake of anything Jane had cooked. But her heart lifted instantly when Jane went on, 'First things first. I'll just make Mr Kershaw a cup of coffee, then I'll—'

Tye was still here! 'I'll do it!' Larch at once volunteered.

'I…' Jane seemed about to protest but perhaps thought it might be a bit of therapy of some sort, and smiled instead.

Larch guessed that Tye was busy at work in the library annexe, but once the coffee was made she began to feel unaccountably shy of taking it in to him. She recalled how, only a few hours ago, he had held her gently in his arms prior to her revealing all the awfulness of her brother-in-law's base actions against her and his wife.

Thinking of Neville Dawson made her shudder. She couldn't go back; she could not. But where else could she go? She pushed all such worries from her. Soon she would part from Tye; she wanted this day, her short time with him, to be harmonious. She wanted good memories—she would face Neville Dawson when she had to.

With Tye uppermost in her thoughts, she placed the coffee on a tray and carried it from the kitchen, along the hall and to the library. Tye was busy at work, and her heart fluttered at just seeing him.

'Don't get up,' she said, but it was too late. He was already on his feet and coming to take the tray from her.

'You didn't have to...' he began.

'I know,' Larch answered. 'Jane would have brought it, but I'm used to being busy. Well,' she qualified, 'before I came here and started to lead a life of utter idleness.'

She turned and was about to go when Tye suddenly stopped her dead in her tracks. 'We can change all that,' he informed her. She turned, looking at him, a question in her look.

'We—can?' she queried slowly.

'I have a job for you.'

Her wide eyes widened. Did he...? Was he...? 'You're offering me a job in your London office?' she asked, the idea having immediate appeal, if only so she would not totally deprive herself of seeing him again.

'I don't think you're ready to return to a full-time job,' Tye confused her by saying, but began to clear some of her confusion by explaining, 'Until Miles gives you the "all clear" to start work again, I thought perhaps next week or the week after—when you feel up to it—you might like to do an hour or so a day cataloguing my grandfather's book collection onto the computer.'

Larch stared at him, her heart drumming in her ears at the wonderful chance Tye was offering her. 'You mean,' she began very carefully, 'that I should stay here while I did the work?'

'It seems more sensible than you trying to find accommodation hereabouts and making your way here daily,' he replied casually—too casually for Larch, who had an enquiring mind. 'Until you have your full strength back you'd be creased by the walk down the drive every morning before you started work,' he added, still in that same casual take-it-or-leave-it tone.

Her pride, which had been well and truly dented because she'd had no other option but to accept so much from him, all at once erupted in full force. 'Some of those books look extremely valuable.' She stood facing him to charge. 'I can't see someone who loved books so much failing to have them already meticulously catalogued.'

'You're right, of course,' Tye agreed mildly. 'But, since I haven't been able to find such a catalogue, now seemed as good a time as any to have them brought up to date and computerised. You're quite nifty with a computer, I believe.'

'Oh, Tye.' She had to laugh to have her words bounced back at her. 'But—working just an hour or so a day it would take me simply ages to have all these books recorded!'

'Did I say there was a time limit?'

She shook her head. 'I can't.'

'Can't what?' He looked determined, and as if he just did not recognise the word 'can't'.

'I can't work for you. I have to go home—today.'

'You'd go back to that house, to that man who is ultimately responsible for you lying in hospital half dead?'

Larch did not know about 'half dead'. Although perhaps being lifeless in a coma came close. She shook her head and, the conversation over, took a step back as she explained, 'You have done so much for me already, Tye. I just cannot take advantage of you any longer.' Oh, she wanted to stay, wanted to catalogue those books, wanted to catalogue them for as long as it took—even if it took for ever. 'You've been so good, so kind, but you must see that—that I can't impose on your kindness any longer. I'll—'

'Nonsense!' Tye cut in shortly—and that annoyed her. 'Your place is here, where you can be looked after!' he rapped.

'I'm not a parcel to be looked after!' she flew, hardly knowing where such temper came from—she'd never used to have much of a temper before. But then she had never been in love before, and was afraid she would give in and stay when pride and everything else decreed that she go.

'You'd prefer to go where that apology for a man can get his lecherous hands on you the moment your sister is out of the way?'

Tye looked tough, talked tough, and Larch, who had never seen him like this, started to feel she might be losing a battle here. 'I have to go! Hazel will come for me as soon as I contact her, and—'

'Good!' Tye chopped her off. And, while Larch stood looking at him, wondering what that 'good' had been all about, he totally shattered her by adding, 'I should like to meet your sister.'

'W-why?' Larch stammered, starting to grow wary; that tough look about Tye was beginning to get to her.

And a moment later she knew she was right to be wary when Tye coolly stated, 'I think it's more than high time someone told her of the criminally licentious antics her husband gets up to when she's not there.'

Larch's mouth fell open. 'You—wouldn't!' she gasped faintly.

Tough was not the word for it, when, 'Try me!' Tye retorted harshly, 'just try me!' Larch stared at him utterly horrified—she knew he was not joking!

CHAPTER SIX

SECONDS ticked by as Larch stared at Tye in wordless stupefaction. 'You...' she gasped when she had her breath back—and was suddenly outraged. 'I told you what I did in complete confidence!' she erupted hotly.

'So sue me!' He was unrepentant.

'You wouldn't. You wouldn't truly tell Hazel?' Her fury had faded a little, a hint of trying to reason with him in her tones.

Tye was unyielding. 'Oh, I would,' he replied, everything about him saying she had better believe it.

'But...' Again she was furious. 'You'd ruin my sister's marriage because...?'

'Your sister *has* a marriage?' he cut in aggressively, and Larch could see that there was just no arguing with the man.

'I can't take any more from you, Tye.' She tried another tack. 'I have to go home. You've done so much for me...'

'So here's your chance to repay me.'

She stared at him mulishly. 'It isn't a proper job,' she challenged. 'You've invented it to—' She broke off again. 'Why would you invent a job? For my pride? To save my pride?' She searched for a reason. 'Why would you? You've done more than enough. If you hadn't happened to be calling on Miles at the hospital that day I was brought in you would never have known me.'

'It was because I was at the hospital, because I saw you when you were rushed in, because I've witnessed the battle you've had since, that I can't have you sliding backwards. You've made excellent progress in the week you've been here. I have absolutely no intention of letting you go back

112

to where that man can prey on you and your emotions and so impede your recovery to full health.'

'But...' She was weakening; she knew that she was. The thought of just seeing Neville Dawson again sickened her.

'But nothing,' Tye said, but his tone had softened. 'Tell me, are you unhappy here?'

'Oh, Tye, you know I'm not.'

He looked pleased with her answer, but was not letting up when he suggested, 'Just look at it logically. You were going to find alternative accommodation from your home anyhow. This way you don't have to wait until you're physically up to all that involves—flat-hunting, moving in, keeping house. On your own admission you're used to being busy—that tells me you're either going to be looking for another job, or taking steps towards that career training you spoke of. Here, believe me—' he glanced around the shelves '—these books really do need to be computer-catalogued.'

'I might make a mess of it,' she attempted.

'I don't believe that for a moment,' he denied, his charm starting to sink her.

'Hazel's not going to like it.'

'Let me talk to her,' Tye suggested.

'I'm keeping you two a mile apart!' Larch exclaimed, not likely to give him a chance to breathe a word of the confidences she had shared with him. He grinned. He could afford to. He knew he had won, as did she. 'When do I start?' she asked. Might as well admit defeat.

He accepted victory with a kind look. 'We'll see how you feel next week.'

Larch made up her mind that by next Monday she would be fully fit.

She left him to drink his coffee and, in her endeavour to get 'fully fit', went out of the house and took a walk alone up to the very end of the long drive. She found, for all her pride not to be a burden to Tye, that she was smiling.

She was not smiling when at five that late afternoon she

began to feel anxious about what she would say to Hazel when she phoned her. She knew what she was *not* going to say to her. In fact Neville Dawson's name was not going to pass her lips if she could help it. Because her sister had always looked out for her, Larch could not see her mildly accepting that she'd had a bit of an accident, was better, but was staying on in the home of the man who had taken it upon himself to give her shelter, without asking some very forthright questions.

It was just after six when Tye came and joined Larch in the drawing room. 'You're looking a little strained,' he observed, coming over to where she was seated on one of the sofas.

Did the man miss nothing? 'I'm rehearsing what to say to my sister when I speak to her.'

'You think she'll be back now?'

'I think there's a good chance.'

His answer was to go and bring the phone over to her. 'Ring her,' he suggested. 'You'll feel better once it's done.'

She hesitated. 'I need help here. What shall I say?'

'Since you seem determined to not tell her the truth, stick as close to the truth as you can,' he advised.

Larch thought he might leave her to it. But, whether or not he had an idea she would stay dithering if he went she did not know, but stay he did. She dialled—and all her rehearsed phrases fell apart when she heard the anxiety in her sister's voice.

'Where are you?' Hazel demanded the moment she knew who it was.

'I'm all right,' Larch quickly assured her.

'I can hear that! Where are you? Aunt Ellen was completely mystified when I rang ten minutes ago and asked to speak to you. She said she hasn't seen a glimpse of you in the weeks it's been since Neville says you walked out on your job. This isn't like you, Larch. What's been happening. I was just about to ring the police and report you missing!'

'I'm sorry you've been worried.'

'I only got in fifteen minutes ago. Neville never said a word about you quitting your job until now—just that you'd gone to stay with Aunt Ellen for a while.'

'I intended to go and stay with Aunt Ellen, I think.' Oh, help, she was useless at subterfuge; she hadn't meant to add those last two words.

As suspected, Hazel missed little. 'You *think*?' she queried. 'Don't you know?'

'I—um—had a bit of an accident,' Larch had to confess, but added quickly, 'I'm fine now, honestly. I—'

'You had an *accident*!' Hazel sounded winded. 'What sort of an accident?'

'I—er—got hit by a car. I'm sorry,' Larch apologised, knowing Hazel was still suffering—their father had been killed in a car accident at the beginning of the year. 'I'm out of hospital now, and—'

'Oh, my... You've been in hosp... Where are you? I'm coming straight away!'

'I'm not in High Wycombe. I'm in a village called Shipton Ash. It's in Hertfordshire.'

'Hertfordshire!' Hazel exclaimed, then got herself together. 'You'd better give me the full address... Have you had surgery? Why didn't you contact Neville? I would have come home straight away. Did you break—?'

'No, no,' Larch assured her. 'Not a break in sight.' Larch did not think it would make Hazel feel any better if she told her she had lost her memory for a short while. 'And I wouldn't have wanted you to leave your work to come back.' Larch hoped that would do for an explanation of why she had not contacted Neville in all this time to tell him of her accident. 'Er—there's no need for you to drive all this way. I mean, if you've only just got in from Denmark...'

'I'm coming to bring you home!' Hazel announced, no two ways about it.

Oh, grief. Larch started to panic. Tye would tell Hazel

exactly why he did not want her to go back to her home in Warren End; Larch knew that he would.

'I'm—er—not ready to—er—come home yet,' Larch said as quickly as she could.

'You're in some kind of cottage hospital, convalescent home?' Hazel asked faintly. 'Just how badly are you hurt?'

'I told you, I'm fine now. Just—um—taking things gently for a little while.'

'I'll come and see for myself,' Hazel determined, as perhaps Larch had known that she would.

'You must be tired.'

'I'm still coming.'

'Er—could you—bring some of my clothes, do you think?'

'Where are you?'

'The house is called Grove House,' Larch supplied.

'What sort of house is it?'

Larch knew she meant was it some kind of medical establishment. 'It's just an ordinary house,' Larch replied, feeling herself go pink—it was a vast house. Her eyes caught Tye's glance on her. He smiled encouragingly.

'Who owns it?'

Oh, grief, Hazel! Tye was sitting there listening and Hazel was like a terrier, but then Larch supposed she had known that too. 'It's owned by a Mr Tyerus Kershaw. He's been—'

'Tyerus Kershaw of Kershaw Research and Analysis?'

'You know him?' Larch asked in surprise.

'Not personally. He's as straight as a die, though. He at once called in our top auditors on one occasion when a section of the firm he was looking into started to smell a touch less than fragrant. You say you're staying in his house? Is he there?'

'Yes.'

'I'd better have a word with him.'

'There's no need,' Larch replied rapidly, and was greatly relieved when Hazel, for the moment, accepted that.

'You're sure you're all right?'

'Absolutely.'

'Stay that way 'til I get there.'

Larch slowly put down the phone. Then she looked up at Tye. 'Hazel knows of you. You once called in her firm, Berry and Thacker.' Tye did not say anything. 'She said you're as straight as a die, and wanted to have a word with you.'

'But you didn't want her to?'

'Not until I've got your word that you won't breathe a whisper to her about what I told you—about her husband.'

Tye looked back at her, his expression serious. 'Let me put it this way,' he said after a while. 'I promise not to shatter your sister's illusions about the man she married, if you promise never again to live under the same roof as him.'

'That's blackmail!'

'It's any name you choose, Larch,' Tye answered, and, his tone stern, 'I have *your* word that you do not intend to let your sister persuade you to go back with her?'

'I don't appear to have any choice.'

'True,' he replied, and smiled. 'One of us should go and check if there's sufficient of Jane's casserole to feed three. Or...' he paused '...will she come accompanied?' Larch paled at the thought that her sister might ask her husband to come with her. 'Don't worry, I shall be here,' Tye quickly assured her—proof there, if proof be needed, that by no chance was Larch ready to go back to her former home. They both knew it too.

As it turned out Hazel, when she arrived, did not appear to have much of an appetite. 'Oh, Larch!' she cried when Larch opened the door to her. Hazel came forward, giving her a big hug then standing back to look into her rested face. 'If anything, you're looking better than when I last saw you,' she commented. 'What's been happening to you?' she wanted to know.

'Come in and meet Tye,' Larch replied, and turned to the

man who was standing in the hall watching the two. She introduced them, overwhelmingly grateful that Hazel had come alone.

Over the next hour, Larch explained all that had happened after the accident. And Hazel was able to see that it was not so much that Larch had walked out on her job, but that she had not remembered having a job. Larch was grateful to Tye that he allowed her sister to believe that her temporary amnesia had stemmed solely from the car accident and had had nothing whatsoever to do with any emotional crisis she had been going through.

And while at first Hazel was very much alarmed that her younger sister had lain in bed not knowing who the dickens she was, with all the trauma that accompanied that realisation, Hazel gradually came to terms with it.

Yet for Larch, who knew Hazel well, it seemed that Hazel appeared strangely distracted somehow. Watching her, Larch did not think it was solely on her account that every so often Hazel would fleetingly appear to have her thoughts elsewhere.

'Is anything the matter, Hazel?' she asked after some minutes of observing her pushing her food around her plate.

'With me? Not a thing,' Hazel answered brightly. 'When I drove here I was determined you must come home with me,' she admitted. 'But you seem to be making good progress. And—' She broke off, looking a tinge worried.

'I'd like Larch to stay here, if you wouldn't mind,' Tye cut in.

Hazel looked instantly relieved. 'Are you sure?' she asked. 'The thing is, now that I can see Larch is doing so well, I should really go away again. It would mean I won't be around to check she isn't overdoing things. I know, given half a chance, Larch would be thinking of sprucing up the house for Christmas. And, with rest and quiet recommended, it might be better for her to stay here for a little while longer.'

'Larch knows she is more than welcome,' Tye replied urbanely.

Larch, while a touch surprised that Hazel was not insisting she go back with her, was not sure that she cared too much for being spoken of as if she was not there. She opted to follow the trend. 'Tye has offered me a job, cataloguing his library,' she told Hazel.

'I know you like to work, but take things steadily,' Hazel advised. 'When do you see your consultant again?' She was by then acquainted with the fact that Larch's consultant was none other than her host's stepbrother.

'I'm in frequent touch with Miles,' Tye cut in. 'He thinks Larch needs to have a few more weeks' rest before he'll be ready to discharge her as fully fit.'

There seemed little more to discuss and, after going to the car and collecting the case she had packed, Hazel stayed only long enough to take a note of the telephone number of Grove House so she could keep in contact. When she had driven away, Larch decided to go to bed.

'Tired?' Tye enquired.

'A bit,' she admitted.

'It's been a long day for you.'

'Thank you for not telling Hazel.'

'Go to bed,' he said. 'I'll bring your case up.'

It seemed to Larch that after that night she made great strides in regaining her former health. Her body stopped aching, and by the end of that week she was more marching up to the end of the drive than taking a leisurely stroll.

She realised that Tye must have seen her striding out, possibly from a window, at some time. Because on Sunday afternoon, when she was in the throes of thinking she might explore beyond the gates at the end of the drive, he came and found her and suggested they might take a short walk.

'You've been reading my mind,' she accepted, and loved him to pieces when, after changing into a reefer jacket and trousers her sister had brought, Larch strolled with Tye around the tiny village.

It was a pretty village, and she knew that she would not at all mind living there permanently. She abruptly brought her mind away from such thoughts. Whatever she did, she must not start to get too familiar with that idea. Soon, she knew, she was going to have to part from Tye. She did not want to. Heaven alone knew that she did not want to. She wanted to be close by him for ever.

She was sorry when, all too soon, Tye guided her to a turning that would bring them back to Grove House. Just being out with him was a joy. It seemed incredible that just a simple walk around the village should give her so much pleasure. Though, as she was well aware, the key words there were 'with him'.

'I enjoyed that,' she told him honestly as they entered the house.

He stood observing her. 'It's brought a touch of colour to your cheeks,' he commented with some satisfaction, and, as if he just could not help himself, he bent and touched his lips to hers.

Larch did not know who was the more startled. Her heart was fairly thundering. 'I…' she murmured on a stray found breath.

Tye abruptly took a step back. 'Forgive me,' he apologised at once. 'I didn't mean to do that. Um—we're going to have to blame it on your lovely colour.'

She had somehow known, without him saying so, that he had not meant to kiss her. Perhaps he was embarrassed that he had. She wanted to help him. 'Think nothing of it,' she said lightly.

'You'd better go and rest,' Tye said shortly—and strode away.

Larch saw little of him in the week that followed. If he had been deliberately avoiding her he could not have been more successful. He had worked from home on Monday, spending long hours in the library annexe, where the phone seemed to ring constantly. He had stayed away overnight on Tuesday and, despite Larch's protest, arranged for Jane to come and sleep overnight.

'I shall be fine on my own!' Larch had tried to argue.

He would have none of it. 'It's all arranged,' he answered shortly, and had business elsewhere of more importance, it seemed. Larch glared at his departing back.

'It seems unfair you have to be uprooted!' Larch remarked to Jane as they sat watching television on Tuesday evening.

'I enjoy coming here,' Jane protested. 'I've been like a fish out of water since old Mrs Kershaw died. Coming here gives me something to do, an aim.'

Hazel was back in Denmark, but telephoned without fail every evening. Larch wanted to confide in her about her love for Tye, but found that she could not. It was much too private.

The love she had for him began to create an ache in her heart when she saw little of him on Wednesday and Thursday. He came home around eight on Friday but seemed so brusque that her pride started to rear up.

That same pride began to soar out of control when, having held back dinner hoping he would arrive some time that night, conversation over the meal was sparse. When, dinner over, she began to clear the table only for him to snarl, 'Leave that!' her pride and anger went roaring into orbit.

'I didn't ask to stay here, remember!' she exploded, and, tears spurting to her eyes, she slammed the dishes back down on the table and shot from the dining room.

She did not make it as far as the bottom of the beautiful staircase before Tye caught up with her. Caught up with her and took a hold of her arms, turning her to face him. Serious grey eyes searched into shining blue ones.

'Don't cry,' he said, a kind of a hoarse note there in his voice. 'Please don't cry.'

'I won't—if you stop being such a complete pig!' she retorted pithily, but immediately started to feel ashamed. Clearly, tough though he could be at times, Larch realised that Tye could not bear to see a woman in tears. Suddenly she folded completely. 'I'm sorry,' she apologised. 'You've had a busy day; you don't need this.'

His answer was to give her a gentle smile and then, as though he could not help it, 'Aw, come here,' he said, and took her in his arms.

It was bliss, pure and simple, to be hugged by him, to be held up against him, but she dared not relax. She loved him and he must never know, but would know if she held on to him as she so sorely wanted to. She pulled back and Tye immediately let her go. 'I never used to be like this—argumentative, snappy,' she said, taking a small step backwards, denying her need to take a big step forwards. 'Do you think that blow to my head released some kind of cross-tempered streak?' She did not expect him to answer, knowing herself that her suddenly new mixed-up temperament stemmed solely from falling heart and soul in love with him and, as a result, being hyper-hyper-sensitive to the smallest hurt, real or imagined, from him.

'You're in recovery, Larch,' he answered seriously. 'Your world had started to cave in before your accident. You're doing well,' he said, and added, 'And I'm a brute.'

She wanted to deny any such thing, but, as ever, was sensitive that she might unthinkingly somehow reveal her true feelings for him. So she grinned cheekily instead, and told him, 'At last we agree on something.' And when, after a small taken aback moment, he laughed, she stepped forward and, totally because she could not help it, stretched up and kissed him. She was at once staggered and quite appalled at her lack of control. Good grief, what had got into her? 'Quits,' she cried, and, hoping with all she had that he would think she was paying him back for kissing her last

Sunday, she turned hurriedly about and went quickly up to her room.

The weekend was no exception to Hazel telephoning her. 'I'm still in Denmark,' she said when she rang on Sunday.

'There's no need to ring every day,' Larch assured her, 'I'm fine.'

'I know,' Hazel replied, and Larch knew she would call her just the same.

She knew how lucky she was to have a sister like Hazel. Briefly Larch thought of her sister's husband, of his betrayal of her dear sister, and felt so badly that she should tell her—but knew that she never would. Hazel loved him, she deserved better, but what good would it do to cause her pain?

Tye started out for London so early on Monday morning that Larch was only out of bed in time to see the rear lights of his car as he went up the drive. He appeared to have made Grove House his present home, but she had no idea for how much longer that would continue before his London home would once again become his main address. All Larch hoped, as she came away from the window and went to shower, was that he would be coming home to Grove House that night.

For her part, she was feeling so well now that she knew another day spent in enforced idleness would send her potty. There was a restless energy in her as she went down the stairs that would not allow her to settle quietly to read or take a walk. And with Mrs Lewis there to do the housework, and Jane refusing to allow her to do anything major in the kitchen, Larch went and got herself some breakfast. She knew that today would see her making a start on that mammoth task of recording the books in the library onto the computer.

By nine-thirty she had the computer ready for action. What seemed like five minutes later, but which turned out to be eleven o'clock, Jane came looking for her.

'So this is where you've got to!'

'I'm having a splendid time,' Larch replied. She had no clue how one went about cataloguing a library of books, but had worked out a very clear and precise system she was happy with.

Jane smiled at her enthusiasm. 'I'll bring you some coffee. Unless you want a break?'

Larch would have been happy to work while she had her coffee. But quite a number of the books she was handling were old and valuable. She would never forgive herself if she spilt so much as a tiny drop of coffee on one of them.

After her coffee she returned to the library and worked solidly until one, when Jane again appeared and advised a break for a sandwich, and in her opinion a rest that afternoon.

While admitting, but only to herself, that she did feel just a tinge fatigued, Larch felt she had spent sufficient time resting and opted to take a walk. 'I'll come with you,' Jane volunteered.

It was the start of a wonderful week as far as Larch was concerned. Hazel phoned early every evening from Denmark and sounded less distracted than she had, which pleased Larch.

Tye came home every evening and seemed pleased to see her. She had mentioned that she had spent an hour or so borrowing his computer but, having been instructed not to do too much, agreed that she would not. She was more interested in his work, and was thrilled when he selected some of the lighter moments to share with her.

By Friday, however, it was beginning to chip away at Larch that, since she was feeling so well now, she had no possible excuse to linger on at Grove House. Those same thoughts preoccupied her when, after being called away by Jane to have her lunch, Larch returned to the library to put away a collection of books she had left on the library table. She was perched on a fascinating set of steps on wheels, replacing the books she had taken down, her thoughts a mixture. She was in the middle of thinking that this job which she felt certain Tye had invented purely to save her pride did not go anywhere near to repaying him for all his kindness to her, when, as she was dwelling on his many kindnesses, the library door suddenly opened. And Tye stood there—looking anything but kind!

'What the devil do you think you're doing?' he charged furiously.

'You're early! I didn't expect you back yet,' she answered innocently.

'Obviously!' he snarled, and, striding over to where she was perched, 'Come down from there at once!' he demanded.

'I'm only...'

'Now!' he barked.

What had she done, for heaven's sake? 'Since you ask so nicely,' she dared bravely, but blanched when his hands came to the steps and he looked angry enough to physically yank her down. 'I'm coming, I'm coming!' she cried, followed by a wobbly kind of, 'Oh-er-wo...' when, with a couple of books in one arm, she found coming down one-handed was not so easy as coming down empty-handed— and she started to slip.

The books went sailing through the air and Tye made a grab for her—about all he could do when it became all too apparent that to do nothing would leave her crashing head-first onto the table. From being flightless to in flight, to safe and secure all in one second, took her breath. But Tye's speedy grip on her was awkward, and her feet were dangling in the air when she began to slide downwards in his hold.

Somehow, probably more in his haste to catch her than to bother where he caught her, his hands were beneath her light sweater. She continued to slip, but as she was sliding down so his grip was sliding up, and from trying to hang on to her ribcage suddenly Larch became aware that Tye had his hands on her breasts. She was momentarily stunned to feel his hands firmly cupping her breasts, and just stared speechlessly at him.

Then all manner of emotions were breaking in her, and in the next moment she had gone a furious red. 'Take your hands off me!' she yelled.

Before she could blink Tye let go of her and her feet abruptly hit the floor. He did not move, other than to take his hands from beneath her sweater, but stayed close and endeavoured to calm her. 'You've got nothing to—'

'Don't you dare touch me!' she hurled at him.

'My dear, I…' Tye tried again. But as swiftly as her panic had arrived, so it as swiftly disappeared, and she could not apologise fast enough.

'Oh, Tye, I'm so sorry!' she apologised, almost tripping over her words in her rush, memory flooding in of just how much she could trust him. This man would never harm her. For heaven's sake, had she so soon forgotten that night when everything had become too much for her and the way she had climbed into his bed? He had held her close through the rest of that night, for her comfort, not his. Sex had just not come into it. 'I'm sorry,' she repeated rapidly, 'so sorry. I don't know what came over me.'

Tye stared at her, up close but no longer touching her. He was studying her, and looked slightly worried. 'Has what happened to you made you afraid of men?' he questioned. He seemed then to lose some of his colour. 'Are you afraid of me?' he asked, and seemed very much shaken at the very thought.

'No—no, of course not. Not you.' She felt it was urgent that he should know. 'I trust you implicitly,' she stated quickly. He did not look totally convinced. 'Honestly, Tye,' she went on, 'I don't know what was in my head to make me panic.' And she tried hard to explain. 'I suppose there might have been a stray thread of memory of Neville Dawson and what he tried to…in there somewhere. But you're nothing like him.'

'I'm glad to hear it,' Tye answered, but he was still watching her, and appeared to be still wondering if she had been permanently damaged by her brother-in-law's assault on her.

'And I suppose—well, to be absolutely truthful, I—er—I'm not familiar with—er—' She broke off. She didn't want Tye stern like this, worried like this, so she continued, 'With men being familiar with my person, either accidentally or on purpose. I—um—suppose it was a bit of a shock.'

Tye's stern expression did not let up. 'You're—totally inexperienced?' he questioned slowly.

She could feel her hot colour returning, but mumbled, 'Yes,' and, feeling awkward suddenly, 'Can I have a hug?' she asked.

And, at that proof of her absolute trust in him, the stern and worried look went from Tye. He put his arms around her and she laid her head against his chest and never wanted to be anywhere else. She felt she had come home.

'All right?' Tye asked after some moments, and although he appeared in no hurry to let her go, Larch took it that what he was saying was that his hug of comfort was over.

She drew back. 'Absolutely,' she said, and his arms fell to his sides.

Strangely, Tye did not step away, but stayed close, and, looking into her eyes, seemed to want to assure her that she was safe with him. 'You do know that I would never take advantage of your innocence?' he asked seriously.

But Larch did not want him back to being stern and worried again. 'Never?' she asked with an impish smile. And, wanting to make him smile, 'Not even if I begged you?' she asked wickedly.

He did not smile. What he did, after a stunned moment of just looking at her, was to burst out laughing. 'That tongue of yours will get you into serious trouble one of these days,' he warned.

Then, as they looked at each other, all at once neither of

them was laughing. They just stood there, staring into each other's eyes. Then, while still looking into her eyes, Tye bent his head and started to come close. They both had all the time in the world to change their minds, but Larch wanted Tye to kiss her, and she could only suppose, when his lips met hers, that he wanted to kiss her too.

Her heartbeats raced as his arms came about her again, only this time to draw her closer to him not in a hug of comfort but in a warm embrace.

Their kiss, though not passionate, was wonderful as far as Larch was concerned. In fact everything was wonderful—being up this close to Tye, being held so firmly in his superb masculine arms. And she wanted more.

Their kiss came to an end and Tye drew back, but she wasn't moving. 'You're a devil for punishment,' he murmured, and his head came down again.

Oh, Tye, I love you so much, she wanted to tell him, but of course could not, so eagerly gave him her lips again, adoring him. And when he drew her yet closer to him and his kiss deepened, she discovered a need to be even closer to him. She pressed herself to him, and an instant later felt his response, and knew that as she had started to feel a physical need for him, so he had an answering physical need for her.

They seemed to mutually pull apart then. She from shyness at this new world she was dipping her toes into, and Tye to give her an askew look as he gently scolded, 'Allow me to tell you, Miss Burton, that you have the power to put a severe strain on a man's resolve.'

Severe strain or no, it did not prevent him from taking his arms from around her, and Larch knew that there would be no more kissing. But those moments shared with him had been little short of magical. So magical that she could hardly speak.

She did manage to find one word, though. 'Good,' she answered, and even managed to find a grin when, not trusting herself not to beg him to take her in his arms again, she turned from him and sailed dreamily out from the library.

CHAPTER SEVEN

LARCH felt she had never been so truly mixed up as she was in the weekend that followed. 'Let's go for a drive,' Tye suggested on Saturday morning. So in love with him was she, she would have agreed had he suggested they had a go at bungee-jumping. So long as she was with him, nothing else mattered.

Again and again she relived those kisses they had shared. His mouth was stupendous—his mouth on hers spine-melting. He made no attempt over the weekend to kiss her again, however, much as she would have welcomed his kisses, but nor did he pretend it had not happened. Even if he did not actually mention those 'close up and personal' moments, he did, during that drive, refer to his coming home early the previous day.

'I'd asked Jane on my way in how you'd been and she said you'd spent the morning happily busy in the library.' Larch's heart picked up a joyful beat. Did Tye often ask Jane questions about her welfare? Did he care? Of course he doesn't, her saner self scoffed, not in the way you want him to care.

'Jane told you that was where I was?' Larch asked, turning her head to look at him as he watched the road up in front.

'Where you *still* were.'

Uh-oh! 'I'm in trouble, aren't I?'

'You were not supposed to be working even *half* a day! Our agreement was for an hour or so.'

'Was that why you were so furious?'

'That and the fact that I thought you'd have more sense than to go shinning up ladders.'

Larch could feel her newly awakened argumentative streak begin to strain at the leash. But she wanted to enjoy her time with him—she was not going to think about a time when she would no longer be with him. 'I don't want to fight with you, Tye,' she said quietly.

He turned his head to look at her. 'Does that mean you're going to obey my every instruction?' he asked, his mouth starting to pick up at the corners.

'Of course,' she lied.

And at her blatant lie he laughed. Though he sobered to say, 'Promise me you won't go leaping about on ladders unless either Jane or I are in the library with you.'

Larch thought the idea a touch restricting, given that it would be physically impossible to reach some of the top library shelves without some sort of a ladder. But she still did not want to argue, so instead—reasonably, she thought—she asked, 'Why?'

'Because Miles hasn't given you the "all clear" yet. For all we know you could be up ladder and start to feel dizzy. It happens to people who haven't had a head injury. You don't want to hit your head again, do you?'

Recalling that awful desolate time when she'd had no idea who she was, remembering the black panic of despair she had sometimes experienced, Larch had no wish whatsoever to experience it ever again. She most definitely did not want to risk another bang on the head.

'OK—I'll be good,' she promised. 'Do you think I should ring Miles and ask him when he thinks I might be ready to see him? It can't be much longer now.'

'It isn't. You're seeing him at three next Friday.'

'Three on Friday!' she repeating, feeling slightly winded.

'At Roselands outpatients' clinic,' Tye confirmed.

'How long have you known?' she asked, feeling a little startled for all she had said it could not be much longer now before she saw Miles for a final time.

'A few days,' Tye replied.

'You didn't think to tell me?'

'I would have remembered by Friday,' he said, his tone off-hand.

He made it sound as if he had temporarily forgotten, but she had an idea that there was very little he had ever 'temporarily' forgotten.

Though she was to wonder at her own ability to temporarily forget that appointment when, back at Grove House, Hazel rang in the early evening and Larch forgot entirely to tell her sister of her appointment.

Although that could have been put down to the fact that Hazel was still in Denmark when she rang, and not at home where Larch had expected she would be. 'Will you be in Denmark for very much longer?' she asked. Even while wanting to be pronounced fully fit by Miles on Friday, she knew that as soon as he discharged her she really would have to do something about leaving Grove House, about leaving Tye. 'I mean,' she added quickly, unable to take thinking of leaving, 'will you be coming home soon?'

'You're all right?' Hazel asked quickly.

'Of course I am,' Larch told her brightly, and came away from the phone knowing that she was far from all right. Oh, how could she possibly leave? Yet, after Friday, she would have no excuse to stay!

Larch did not sleep well that night, but by morning she had decided that she was not going to think of a time when she would be apart from Tye. That time would come all too soon.

Tye had work he wanted to complete that day, but did find time to tell her to put a jacket on. 'Come for a walk round the village,' he suggested.

She stored up more memories. Standing with Tye on a tiny footbridge. Tye placing an arm about her shoulders while he turned her to draw her attention to a most magnificent red-berry-bearing hollybush. She stood quietly in the shelter of his arm, and although they stayed like that for a while, as though he had forgotten his arm was holding her, he all too soon remembered and removed it.

She had not felt cold before, but she felt cold then. Cold and bleak. The hollybush reminded her that next month would see the arrival of December. She would be back home for Christmas. She did not look forward to it. Home was not home any more. Where would Tye be?

He left for his office very early again on Monday. But when Larch went to start work in the library her heart lifted. The stack of books that had been reposing on the highest shelves had been taken down and were now on the large library table. She felt a glow of love for him. Tye had done that for her.

He returned home just before seven and her spirits lifted just to see him. They had finished dinner when, Jane having gone home, Larch insisted she was quite well enough to wash a few dishes and not leave them for Jane or Mrs Lewis in the morning. For once he allowed that she probably was strong enough, but in turn insisted, 'I'll come and give you a hand.'

'You don't have to!' she protested. 'I'm sure you've got a briefcase full of stuff you'd prefer to be getting on with.'

'You refuse to let me explore my domestic side?'

Larch gave him a speaking look. 'There's no arguing with you,' she retorted sniffily—secretly loving the domesticity of it when he helped her carry their used dishes to the kitchen and he dried while she washed. They were moments to store, to hold, to keep.

They were chatting in a companionable way that warmed her heart when Tye revealed that he would be going away on Wednesday for a few days.

'Oh,' she murmured. Some input was called for from her, but any lifted spirits at once plummeted that by the look of it she would not see him for at least two whole days! Her chilled feelings turned to dread. How on earth was she going to feel when, as must soon happen, she would never see him again?

'You'll be all right,' Tye assured her, perhaps taking that 'oh' for apprehension at the thought of being in the large house all by herself. 'I've already spoken with Jane. She'll be here from Wednesday morning until I get back.'

'There's no need for…'

'I think there is,' he contradicted before she could finish. 'You've come a long, long way from when I saw you first. Aside from the bumps and bruises you collected, the stiffness and pain you endured while your body healed, I know it hasn't been easy for you. A good part of the time it must have been totally nightmarish. But you're almost there now.' He smiled at her. 'Indulge me, Larch,' he requested with charm enough to sink a battle cruiser. 'Let Jane sleep in, then after Friday—' He broke off to smile again before going on, 'I'm probably going to regret this, but, subject to Miles discharging you from his "follow-up" list, I'll allow you to do anything at all you may wish.'

Larch had to smile back at him. 'I might keep you to that,' she answered lightly, adding as casually as she was able, 'Any idea when you'll be back?'

'If you're worrying about your clinic appointment, I'll be back to take you to Roselands.'

'You don't have to,' her pride reared up to state. 'I can—'

'No, you can't. I'll be here by about midday on Friday,' he promised.

'You're cutting your work short because of me,' she accused, feeling dreadful suddenly that through her his work had been disrupted, causing him to catch up evenings and weekends.

'Will you stop feeling guilty?' he requested good-humouredly. 'I promise you my work is not suffering, nor has it suffered in any way. In fact,' he went on, 'my business has gone from strength to strength.'

'But…'

'But nothing. I'll be here to take you to see Miles,' he reiterated firmly.

She was still feeling guilty, but rather than argue with him, this man she loved, said 'If you're sure—'

'I'm sure,' he cut in, and was looking steadily at her when he added quietly, 'I'm looking forward to it.'

Before she had a chance to analyse that remark, or to wonder or indeed decide if there was anything to analyse, the kitchen phone rang and Tye walked over to answer it. 'Larch is here,' he said, and asked a pleasant, 'How are you?' before turning to hold out the phone to Larch. 'It's your sister.'

'Hello, Hazel,' Larch greeted her brightly, and they chatted about matters inconsequential for a few minutes, until Larch asked, 'You're still in Denmark?'

'I'm coming home this weekend,' Hazel replied. 'I—' She broke off. 'It doesn't matter. I'll tell you when I see you,' she said.

'Sounds important?'

'Stop fishing,' Hazel laughed.

'You've got another promotion and...?'

'So tell me what you've been doing.' Hazel refused to be drawn. 'You're keeping well? You haven't...?'

'I'm fine,' Larch assured her. 'Actually, I'm going for my final check-over on Friday.'

'Don't count your chickens.'

'Now who's the mother hen?' They both laughed, and ended the call—Hazel, Larch presumed, to do some more studying.

'Your sister has a promotion?' Tye asked as Larch replaced the phone.

Nothing like blatantly listening in. Though, since he was in the same room, Larch realised that there was not very much else he could do. 'It sounds very much as though she has,' Larch replied. 'Hazel works hard enough. She has something to tell me, anyhow, but refuses to tell me until she comes home this weekend.'

In her bed that night when, as was usual now, Larch re-lived every moment shared that evening with Tye, she re-called his 'I'm looking forward to it' comment. Did he mean he was looking forward to Friday when Miles would pro-nounce her as fit as a flea so Tye could say, Goodbye, it's been nice knowing you?

She paled at the thought that Tye could not wait to be rid of her. Then she recalled how he had insisted that she stay at Grove House until she was well again, and she began to feel a touch better. But that was only until she realised that she *was* well again now—so what was she hanging around for?

Love, she was on to realising, after going through yet another gut-tearing gamut of emotions, played the very devil with one's instincts, one's sensitivity. In fact love, her love for Tye, was making her doubt her own shadow. She would be a nervous wreck if she kept this up.

Larch finally fell asleep, but only after she had firmly decided that she was not going to look under the stones of everything Tye said. While she supposed it was true that he seldom said anything he did not mean, she would drive her-self scatty if she started to dissect every throwaway utter-ance he ever made. From now on, she determined, she would take all and everything he said at face value. Therefore 'I'm looking forward to it' meant just that. He was looking forward to taking her to the clinic on Friday because… Oh, stop it. You're doing it again. Stop it.

For all the doubts that had plagued her during the dark hours, Larch was in the window seat in her room early the next morning to watch Tye's car disappear up the drive. Face value, she reminded herself as she stood under the shower.

She had breakfast and started work in the library, smiling to see yesterday's books had miraculously sailed back up to their appointed shelves, and that there was a fresh stack of books now reposing on the library table.

It was just before twelve when Larch left the computer to return another batch of books to the library table and heard a car come roaring up the drive. Jane never drove like that! Larch glanced out of the window to see an expensive-looking car pull up at the front door. Moving to the side of the window, Larch continued to watch as an elegant and well-dressed woman of about forty left the car and approached the front door.

With the recovery of her memory it was no longer important for someone to be in the house with her at all times. Consequently, while Jane was on hand a lot of the time, more now as cook—a job she revelled in—than anything, she was not expected for a while.

The doorbell rang. Larch had no idea who the caller was, but saw no reason not to answer it. She went from the library and along the hall, and had just reached the front door when the bell rang again.

'Ah!' the woman exclaimed as Larch pulled back the stout oak door. 'You *are* in!' She smiled a friendly smile, but, when Larch did not invite her over the threshold, 'I'm Tye's sister-in-law,' she introduced herself.

'Paulette?' Larch pulled the name from her memory bank, and the attractive older woman seemed exceedingly pleased.

'You've heard of me!' she trilled. 'I know I'm too late for coffee and too early for lunch, but when my husband let slip that Tye had a live-in lover, I got over here as fast as I could.'

Larch's jaw dropped in astonishment. This woman thought she and Tye... Larch did not know which to do first—put the woman straight on that score before they went any further, or to invite her in. 'Come in,' she invited, deciding that this was not a discussion she wanted to have on the doorstep. 'Would you like coffee?' she asked.

'No, no. Thank you all the same. My, this house hasn't

changed much. Not that I came here all that often.' She
laughed suddenly. 'Well, not after old lady Kershaw suggested one time that if I did have to "rattle on", as she put
it, would I please do it elsewhere as I was giving her a
migraine. My heavens, she could be blunt—and that was
without bothering to put her mind to it,' she added with
another laugh.

By that time they had reached the drawing room and
Larch stood back to let her guest, whom she realised, in the
manner of things, had more right there than herself, precede
her into the room.

'Take a seat,' Larch invited pleasantly, and, taking a seat
across from her, waited only until Paulette Phipps was
seated before she at once began to set her straight. Or, at
least, attempted to. 'I don't know what Miles told you—'

'You've met him?' Paulette interrupted.

'Yes, but…'

'Now, isn't that typical! You'd think I was an agent for
Spies Incorporated the little my beloved tells me! Just because I—positively years ago—happened to mention to a
friend a very minor matter, so minor as to be insignificant,
about one of his patients, he now tells me absolutely nothing! It's such a trial,' she said, then laughed an infectious
kind of laugh as she added, 'Thanks be that there's so much
other stuff to gossip about.'

'Which—' Larch attempted to get in—then wondered if
she must have a very quiet voice because Paulette did not
appear to have heard her.

'Miles arranged to have today off—unless of course some
emergency crops up, which of course it will. He was oper-
ating until four this morning, so didn't get up until nearly
eleven.' She 'rattled' enthusiastically away, going on with
amazing breath control since she did not appear to take another breath, 'I wanted to go to a place in town for lunch,
but Miles said he just wanted to potter about and relax.
Well, you know how it is. I wanted to be up and doing and

he, poor sweetie, wanted to stay home to unwind. So, purely to give him some time to himself, while at the same time not being too far away—we spend so little time together as it is,' she threw in, not laughing, but beaming, 'I said I'd find something else to do.'

Larch, who up until then had led a reasonably quiet life, was finding her visitor's personality a touch swamping. She had a feeling she should try and stop this friendly but gabbling woman from revealing anything further. She doubted Paulette would be so open if she knew that Larch's relationship with her stepbrother-in-law was not as she imagined. Or would she? Larch was suddenly unsure. Though she was determined she would set her straight about her relationship with Tye any second now.

'I know your husband works very hard,' she attempted, as a prelude to telling her just how she knew that and then going on to the reason why she was, for the moment, residing at Grove House.

'Tell me about it!' Paulette took up. 'Anyhow, where was I? Oh, yes.' Again she did not pause for breath. 'So there was I, thinking to make myself scarce, but not too scarce— I idolise the man,' she said with another of her laughs. 'So I told Miles, You potter, darling. I think I'll go and take a look at Grove House. I mean, with Tye always so busy, it could have been a positive age since anyone had been to take a look—squatters could have moved in or anything. Until Tye decides what he's going to do with the place somebody has to keep an eye on it. But imagine my surprise when Miles said I mustn't come anywhere near Grove House. Naturally I wanted to know why!'

'Naturally,' Larch responded faintly.

'Well, you can imagine my surprise that, when pushed, Miles told me I must stay away because Tye had a house guest. House guest? I ask you! As soon as I knew Tye's guest was female I had to come over. I mean, I just never thought I'd live to see the day that Tye took one of his lady-loves to *actually* live with him. He's always been far too wily for that.'

Larch again opened her mouth to tell Paulette Phipps the precise reason why she was Tye's house guest. But to her own surprise heard herself query, 'Wily?'

Paulette gave her a lovely smile, as though to soften her words, but when she started off, 'Forgive me, my dear,' Larch knew she was not going to like what she was going to hear. Nor did she, when Paulette went on, 'But I just never thought Tye would ever put himself in the position where, when the first flush had faded, he might find himself with a problem—depending on her clingability, of course—when he wanted to live—er—unencumbered, as it were. Of course, now that I've seen you I can see that—' A telephone rang; it was Paulette's mobile. 'Excuse me,' she said, and took her phone from her bag.

'Yes,' she said, and, 'Yes,' again. A beaming smile and, 'I'd adore to! Are you sure you don't want to…? All right, darling.' She checked her watch. 'I'll be with you in twenty minutes. What? No, of course not! I wouldn't dream of going anywhere near Grove House.' She ended her call, put her phone away and stood up. 'My husband knows me too well. I bet he thinks I'm on my way here and that by dangling the carrot of the lunch I wanted at my favourite restaurant he thinks I'll forget all about Tye's mistress.' She was already making for the door.

Larch felt a panicky urgency to speedily tell her the true facts. But her visitor was obviously in a rush to go and have lunch with the husband she idolised.

'Do you know, I don't even know your name?' she said as they went hurrying along the hall.

'Larch. Larch Burton,' Larch supplied. 'Paulette…' she began as they reached the front door.

'I'm sorry it was such a short visit. Perhaps we'll do lunch one day?'

'I…'

'Meantime I must fly!' Paulette was through the door and about to get in to her car when she called over its roof to a stunned Larch, 'What's the betting my conscience will get the better of me and before the year's out I confess to that man of mine that I didn't have to go anywhere near Grove House because I was actually there when he rang?' Again Paulette laughed. 'Bye, Larch,' she said, and—foot down, with a roar of the engine—she was gone.

Larch went to the library but was too shattered, too shaken by Paulette's visit, to be able to concentrate on computer work. She still had not resumed when Jane popped her head round the door to enquire if she fancied chicken pie for dinner that evening. 'Are you all right?' Jane asked. 'You look...'

'I'm fine.' Larch quickly got herself together. 'Paulette Phipps called,' she mentioned.

'Ah!' Jane exclaimed, as if that totally explained why she should look so shaken. Life at Grove House had so far been serene and peaceful.

Ah, indeed! A few minutes later, alone once more, Larch went over again everything Tye's stepsister-in-law had said. The thing was that Larch felt she could quite get to like Paulette Phipps. She was open and she was friendly—but Larch could quite understand why Miles told his garrulous wife so little. What she knew, she shared. What she did not know she assumed, and shared that too.

With the words 'mistress' and 'clingability' bouncing around in her head, Larch found it impossible to fully concentrate on what she was doing. She was glad to abandon the library and go and have a sandwich with Jane.

They decided to go for a walk that afternoon, but Larch could not outpace her thoughts, and returned from their walk in mental torment. Was she clinging? Worse, because Tye was good and kind, was she making it impossible for him to say that she was well enough to go?

She went up to her room, her insides churning as doubts

and 'mistress' and 'clingability' continued to bombard her. Demons of doubt had her in their grip, pursued her so that in the end she knew she was going to have to leave. She was not, and never had been, Tye's responsibility. Nor did she wish to be. But—where would she go?

Needing to be busy, but feeling too discomposed to settle to anything very much, she returned downstairs. She peeled and cleaned vegetables for the evening meal and told Jane she could quite well cope with it if she had any plans for the evening.

'Well, if you're sure? There's a meeting of the Christmas bazaar committee tonight. I wouldn't mind checking a few things over before then,' Jane accepted.

Jane was far from Larch's thoughts when at half past six she heard Tye's car on the drive. She felt that she probably ought to mention to him that Miles's wife had called, but she was feeling too bruised to want to start a conversation— the subject being, what the loquacious Paulette had spoken of. Anyhow, since Paulette clearly was not thinking of mentioning her visit to her husband just yet, Tye was not likely to hear of it for quite some while. Bleakly, Larch knew that when that time came she would be long gone.

'Good day?' she asked Tye when he came and found her in the kitchen. She looked over to him, her heart turning cartwheels just to see him.

'Can't complain. How about you?' he asked pleasantly, standing there, briefcase in hand, his eyes on her face.

'The usual,' she lied. 'I told Jane I would see to the meal. What time would you like dinner?' she asked, her tone perhaps a little off-hand in her attempt to counter any suggestion that she might be thought to be 'clinging'.

Tye looked at her for a silent moment or two. 'When it's ready,' he answered, and went from the kitchen—she presumed to shower and freshen up.

Larch tried hard to appear natural when later she and Tye were having dinner. But each time some naturally thought comment would pop into her head she found she was pausing to question it—did that comment sound clinging, or was that the sort of comment a mistress would make?—and the comment never got uttered.

Why it should surprise her that Tye, as observant as ever, should notice that something was slightly amiss she could not have said. But she was taken out of her unhappy thoughts when later, as they stood in the kitchen attending to the used dishes, he quietly asked, 'What's wrong, Larch?'

'Nothing,' she answered quickly.

He did not believe her, and, putting down the drying cloth, he caught hold of her by the shoulders and turned her to face him. 'You're not worrying about Friday?'

You could say that, she supposed, knowing for certain that on Friday she would be leaving Grove House and never coming back—yet still had no earthly idea where she would go. 'Good heavens, no,' she replied. 'I shall pass any test Miles cares to give me with flying colours!'

Tye smiled encouragingly. 'That's the spirit,' he said, adding, 'If you're very good I'll take you for a celebratory dinner afterwards.'

Oh, Tye, don't do this to me! She could think of nothing she would rather do than go out to dinner with him. But he was being kind again, and he deserved better than to have some woman latch on and cling to him.

'I'll be so good you wouldn't believe,' she answered, hoping he would not go to any trouble booking a table. She would not be there.

Together they finished the dishes, and her heart ached at such wonderful domesticity. She found she was glancing at the kitchen clock, almost as if counting the hours until she must part from him.

'Hazel's late,' Tye commented, following her glance.

'I expect she's tied up with something,' Larch replied lightly. Though he was right; her sister had usually phoned by this time.

Larch went with him to the drawing room. She knew that she never ever wanted to part from him, but full well knew that he would be going away tomorrow and the next time she would see him would be Friday, when he came to Grove House to take her to keep her appointment at Roselands clinic. Her emotions started to get out of hand. Mistress, clinging, leaving, never to see him again—all chased each other round in her head. When would she tell him that she would not be coming back to Grove House on Friday? When…?

Abruptly she got out of her chair. She could not take it. 'I think I'll go to bed!' she said jerkily.

'Larch! What is it?'

'I shouldn't think Hazel is going to ring now,' Larch said, speaking quickly, heading for the door.

Before she could get there, though, Tye had somehow managed to get to the door first. He halted her, staring down into her agitated beautiful blue eyes. 'Something's troubling you?' he questioned.

'Not at all!'

'You're sure you're not worrying about the outcome when you see Miles on Friday?'

'Certain. Honestly!' she replied. It was what happened after that, after she parted from Tye, that worried her. How would she cope with not seeing him? 'I'm not worrying about a thing!' she promised, forcing a cheerful note.

He was not convinced. 'You have a headache?' he questioned, not budging an inch from blocking her way out of the door.

'I'm fine. Absolutely. Perhaps just a bit tired,' she lied. Tye studied her for perhaps another ten seconds more, then stood aside and opened the door for her. 'Goodnight,' she said quickly, and slipped through the doorway. She did not look round, would not look round, but she sensed he was still in the doorway as she went swiftly up to her room.

She was not tired and did not want to go to bed. That

was to say, she was not physically tired, but she was oh, so weary of the same spirit-defeating thoughts that tossed around and around in her head.

Eventually she went and showered and got into a night-dress, telling herself she had known anyway that she would soon be leaving. It was just that after Paulette's visit that day the knowledge that she could no longer stay had become set in concrete.

Mistress. Clinging. Had she clung so much that Tye was unable to prise her away? That sinking thought battered at her again and again. As did the knowledge batter her that she had truly spited herself, in that by taking herself off to bed she had done away with any chance to see him again before Friday. She could hardly intrude on his early morning tomorrow, when he would be busy getting ready to go to his office.

Friday! She did not want to think about Friday. Oh, she wasn't worried about seeing Miles. She felt so well now it was a foregone conclusion that he would discharge her from his list. But—what was she going to tell Tye? Would he be relieved? Probably—totally, came back the unwanted answer.

A dry kind of sob took her, and Larch forced herself to concentrate on matters practical. As yet she had no idea what reason she was going to give Hazel for not returning to their old home. Larch knew, now that she was no longer exhausted by her workload and was strong again, that she was just not going to live again under the same roof as Neville Dawson.

Which meant that early tomorrow morning she must get on the phone and start trying to find a bedsit somewhere. It need not necessarily be in High Wycombe, she realised. Since she was set on leaving home, she could live anywhere. Hazel would be a problem; Larch knew that. Given that she had been the one to stay home and look after their mother, it had not prevented Hazel from looking out for her younger sister. It was going to be difficult.

And the most difficult part would be in saying a permanent goodbye to Tye. But, with that hated word 'clinging' refusing to stay out of her head, there was no other way.

Larch was sitting in the window seat in her nightdress and light wrap, her thoughts taken up solely with the man she would next see on Friday but never again after that, when to her surprise he knocked on her bedroom door and after a few seconds came in.

Tye looked serious, and she left the window seat with an idea that she was in trouble over something. He had shed his jacket, but whether he had been working or on his way to bed she did not know. What she did know, as he quietly closed the door and came over to where she was standing, was that he wanted a word with her, obviously over some matter that would not wait until Friday.

He stopped when he was about a yard away from her where, even in the shaded lamp of her bedside light, he could see her expression. 'What...?' she began.

'Exactly!' he said. 'What?' Larch stared at him, realising he looked more kind of coaxing than angry. 'What did Paulette say that upset you?'

'You know she was here today?' Larch exclaimed.

'*You* didn't tell me,' he replied. 'Why not, Larch?'

'It—er...' She had been about to lie and say it had slipped her mind, that she had forgotten his stepsister-in-law's visit. But Tye would not swallow that. Paulette was like a whirlwind—blow in, devastate the area—in this case Larch's peace of mind—and, like a whirlwind, blow out again. Nobody would ever forget Paulette! 'Has she just phoned about something?' Larch asked instead, reasoning that since Tye had not known about Paulette's visit at dinner, and since he had not been outside the house since, he must have heard over the phone.

'Miles rang.' Tye corrected her impression it was Paulette who had made the call.

'Hmm,' Larch mumbled, realising that Paulette had come clean about her visit sooner than anticipated. 'Paulette was only here for a brief while…'

'But in that brief while she managed to upset you?'

'Not at all,' Larch denied. 'I found her a very likeable person.'

'She is,' Tye agreed. 'Deep down she is quite a warm and generous woman. Unfortunately, she's a lady whose portion of tact has been substituted by an Olympian-sized ability to constantly put her foot in it.' Larch felt her lips twitch. She noticed there was a hint of a smile on his superb mouth too. 'So tell me, what particular piece of prime tactlessness did Paulette blithely floor you with today?'

'It wasn't that bad!' Larch felt she should deny it, but realised too late that she had just admitted Paulette had floored her with something.

'So?'

Tye was waiting, his smile not making it. And, while Larch had not the smallest intention of giving him a verbatim report, since he did not look likely to budge until she had told him something, she haltingly revealed, 'Paulette assumed that I—that I was—your—mistress.'

'Oh, Larch,' Tye murmured softly. 'I'm sorry. I never…'

'It's not your fault. Apparently Miles doesn't discuss his patients with her, but he inadvertently let her know you had a guest here.'

'Paulette put two and two together and made her usual dozen.'

'I did try to tell her, but—'

'But you couldn't manage to get a word in,' Tye interrupted, as though he knew exactly how it had been. 'I should have thought to warn you just in case she called—people have been known to dive into hedges when they see her coming,' he inserted, bringing a smile to Larch's mouth. 'It just never occurred to me that she would, as Miles put it just now, think to keep an eye on the place. I'll ring her tomorrow and put her right.'

'You don't...'

'Yes, I do,' he contradicted, and Larch warmed to him—then her smile faded, her sensitivity playing nonsense games with her again. Quite plainly Tye did not want anyone believing he was her lover. 'What have I said?' he asked, his eyes reading her every expression.

'Nothing,' Larch lied. 'I just hope you have better luck than I did.'

'Well, I know I'll have to be quick,' he agreed. And there was a teasing note there when he went on, 'Dear Paulette once had a go at scuba-diving—but had to give it up when she found she just couldn't keep her mouth shut under water long enough to—'

Larch burst into spontaneous laughter before he finished. 'You've just made that up!' she accused.

His mouth curved upwards, and she realised he was purposely trying to make her feel happier. He proved it when he said, 'That's better,' and, suddenly taking a step nearer, he reached for her and gathered her in his arms in a hug of comfort.

Larch knew he meant only to comfort her, to sort of make up for all the worried turmoil she had been in ever since Paulette's visit. But feeling his warmth through his shirt, his body so close, Larch all at once started to lose all perspective. All she knew as Tye held her was that after Friday... But she did not want to think about Friday. Did not want to think... Her arms went around his waist, and as he held her, so she held him.

After a few soul-soothing moments she felt him move, as though to stand away from her. But she did not want that. She held on to him. 'My dear,' he said, in a strangled kind of way.

She looked up. Stood in the circle of his arms and looked

up, not backing away. She looked at his mouth, that wonderful mouth, and wanted him to kiss her. She raised her eyes to his, saw his glance flick to her lips—and guessed when his head started to come down that Tye wanted to kiss her too.

He did kiss her. It was a gentle kiss, but a warm kiss too. He pulled back, but his arms were still around her. 'I should let you go,' he murmured.

'No, you shouldn't,' she answered with a shy smile, and loved it when Tye appeared to need no further invitation than that.

Gently he laid his mouth over hers again, and it was wonderful. Her heart raced, and as the pressure of his mouth over hers suddenly started to increase, so he began to draw her closer to him. Willingly, she went.

'You're beautiful,' he murmured against her ear.

Oh, Tye, I love you so much. She held him closer, stretching up to kiss him, feeling his hands on her through the thin covering of her nightwear. Oh, Tye, Tye. She wanted to call his name as he parted her lips with his own, a thrill of pure delight shooting through her when she felt the tip of his tongue on her lips.

'Oh, Tye,' she cried involuntarily.

His answer was to pull back again, as though to check all was well with her. Her answer was to reach up, to kiss him, and to touch his lips with the tip of her tongue.

His response was all she could have hoped for. His arms tightened about her, and then he was kissing her in a way she had never imagined, thrilling her anew as his hands caressed over her back, drawing her yet closer to him.

He held her in the firm hold of one arm while one hand caressed tenderly to the front of her. She made a small swallowing sound when gently he captured one of her breasts. He heard it. 'Are you all right with this?' he asked throatily, sensitive fingers sending her mindless as he teased and tormented the hard peak of her breast. 'Do you want me to stop? Say now,' he demanded, his tone urgent.

'Don't stop! Don't stop,' she cried, and was glad when his mouth triumphantly claimed hers again, because she had so very nearly added just how much she loved him.

She had thought their kisses could not get much more passionate, but knew she had a lot to learn when the next time he kissed her he aroused such a vortex of feeling in her.

She felt her thin wrap fall to the floor and cared not; she was a willing pupil. He bent and traced feather-light kisses over her shoulders, moving the fine straps aside from first one shoulder and then the other. She felt her nightdress start to slip down and away from her, and experienced a belated moment of modesty, so clutched at it, holding it to her.

A modesty she forgot a minute later when she knew an urgent desire to touch his skin. She freed her arms from her straps and began to unbutton his shirt. 'Am I being forward?' she asked shyly, and he laughed in delight.

'We have been introduced,' he assured her softly, and undid the rest of the buttons himself.

He had a most magnificent chest, she observed a few seconds later, her heart drumming in her ears, his shirt now reposing on the floor. She wanted to kiss his dark hair-bestrewn, hard-muscled broad chest. And did. 'Oh, Tye,' she murmured in awe, and just had to taste his nipple.

'Fair's fair,' he breathed as she raised her head, and he bent to first kiss her lips and trace tender kisses over her throat and shoulders, then he moved the material of her nightdress down and took the peak of her left breast inside his moist mouth.

She was in a no man's land of wanting, pressing against him, his mouth doing mindless things to her. At which point her nightdress started to slip, and quickly fell to the floor. 'Tye!' Larch exclaimed faintly, and knew he had picked up the faint note of panic when he took his lips, his tongue, from her breast and raised his head.

'I'm frightening you?' he queried tenderly.

'No!' she denied. 'No, not at all. It's just…'

And she loved him when he smiled a gentle smile and understood. 'This is all so new to you, isn't it, my darling? And I'm going too fast.'

'It's—it's wonderful—really,' she protested softly.

But he had taken a small step back—small, but far enough that when he glanced down he was able to see her body in its entire nakedness. 'Oh, my dear, dear, Larch. You are exquisite,' he breathed. Then he glanced up to her face—and saw it was aflame with colour. He stared into her eyes, then a dull tide of colour came up under his skin too. 'I'd—better go,' he said, his voice all kind of thick in his throat.

Go! She could not have that. In the next second Larch had covered the small space between them, thrilling anew as her naked breasts touched his bare skin. She pressed closer, her breasts firm against his chest.

'Kiss me!' she whispered, and heard him groan—then his mouth was against hers, one arm around her waist, a hand cupping her buttock, sending her into raptures as he pulled her against him.

She knew then how desperately he wanted her. And it was wonderful, because she wanted him too, quite as desperately. Again he began to part her lips with his, and she clung on to him, mindless of all and anything but the enchanted world that he was taking her to.

Then all at once Tye was breaking that kiss. 'No!' She heard that faint strangled sound, and incredibly he was pulling away from her, his hands coming to her upper arms, gripping her as if he needed some strength, as if he needed something to hold on to. Iron bands clamped on to her, held her from him as he tried not to look down at her delicious breasts, and the sweet curve of her belly, and the magnet of her thighs. 'No!' he said again, and as if trying to convince himself he shook his head. 'No. I'm sorry,' he added on a kind of despairing sound, his hands falling away from her.

And while, open-mouthed, stunned and disbelieving, Larch followed him with her eyes, Tye, not waiting for anything, certainly not pausing for so much as a split second to pick up his shirt, went striding from her room.

CHAPTER EIGHT

IT WAS a long night. By morning Larch knew one thing without fear of contradiction, and that was that Tye—no matter how much his body might have desired her body—had no time for clinging women.

And, remembering just how clinging she had been, Larch wished herself a thousand miles away from Grove House. She recalled how all Tye had meant to do at the start was to give her an unsexual kind of hug because he'd known she was upset. He had even tried to get away, and what had she done? She had only clung onto him, that was all!

She groaned in mortification. 'I should let you go,' he had said. 'No, you shouldn't,' she had replied. Larch buried her head under the bedcovers as though trying to hide from the determined knife-stabbing onslaught of her memories. She was glad she was not going to have to see him until Friday. The way she was feeling—Friday would be too soon.

Unable to rest, Larch sat up and, needing something to cheer her, switched on her bedside lamp. She had two whole days to get herself back together again before she saw Tye. She had an idea that two days would not be nearly enough.

But she did not have even that much time. Because just then there was a knock on her door and, totally unexpectedly, dressed in a business suit and plainly on his way out, possibly to keep some business appointment, Tye came in.

Her heart went into overdrive, and as she recalled the way she had last night stood naked in front of him scorching hot colour burned her skin. Tye came over to her bed, his eyes on her riotous blush, and, looking down at her, 'Hate me?' he asked softly.

And she wished that he hadn't, because it was another instance of why she loved him so much. She was at fault—and he was taking the blame! 'I shall need notice of that question.' She somehow managed a prim note, but found a smile so he should know she was not so much affected.

Tye perched on the edge of her bed and took a hold of her hand. 'I'm not going to apologise,' he said, his grey eyes fixed on hers.

Apologise? Suddenly it came to Larch what he was talking about. He meant did she hate him for making love to her, making her want him so, but only to walk out on her? 'One of us had to be sensible,' she mumbled, but could feel herself going red again.

'Oh, Larch,' Tye said gently. 'Don't be embarrassed. These things happen. But I've more experience—I shouldn't have let it happen.'

How could he blame himself? She had been the one to cling on to him, not the other way around! 'Well, don't let it happen again,' she said severely, and they both laughed, then stilled—and her heart thundered when she thought from the look in his eyes that he was going to kiss her again.

But he did not. He just gave the hand he was holding a squeeze. 'Be good,' he instructed, and, standing, added, 'I'll see you on Friday,' and was gone.

Weak tears sprang to her eyes. He had not been going to kiss her, nor would he ever again. And she loved him, and she would soon be leaving, and she would never see him again—and she couldn't bear it.

Larch showered and dressed with her head filled with thoughts of Tye, with thoughts of how, on Friday, she would leave Grove House for the last time. She would have to tell Tye she was not coming back—though he would know that when he saw her suitcase.

She made her bed and tidied her room—and came near to tears again when she picked up his shirt, the one she had helped to unbutton last night. She held it against her cheek for countless seconds while she strove for control.

Going downstairs, she made a pot of tea and tried to instil in herself some sense of purpose, some kind of energy. Hadn't she decided to spend that morning phoning round to find a bedsit she could move into come Friday? She had little idea of her expected finances, Hazel would be dealing with all that, but, apart from the pittance Neville Dawson had paid her, she had a small amount in her savings account. She would have enough to afford some modest hotel for a week or two if she were unable to find rented accommodation straight away.

Perhaps she would find somewhere in the Hertfordshire area? She was just scolding herself for the thought, for wanting to stay in the same county where Grove House was situated, when someone rang the front doorbell.

Hoping against hope that the caller was not Paulette Phipps—Larch did not think she was up to Paulette's lively chatter that morning; it was only a little after eight, for goodness' sake!—Larch reached the door with Tye in her head again, realising that he might well decide to sell Grove House, so should she opt for Hertfordshire that would rule out any faint possibility of ever accidentally bumping into him anyway.

She pulled open the stout front door and was dumbfounded to see her sister standing there. 'Hazel!' she exclaimed. 'I thought you were in Denmark.' And in the following ten minutes she had something other than Tye to focus on.

'I came home last night,' Hazel replied.

'Come in. Have you had breakfast?'

Hazel shook her head and stepped over the threshold. 'Tye's not here, I suppose?' she asked as they went along the hall towards the kitchen, as if she expected any businessman would be up and on his way to his office by this time.

'He's away on business for a few days,' Larch replied.

In the kitchen she set the kettle to boil and turned to hear Hazel blurt out in a rush, 'I needed to see you urgently. It wouldn't wait.'

'Something's the matter?'

'Not now,' Hazel replied. 'Things have been a little, well, murderous, I suppose you could say. But everything's more or less fine now.' Then quite out of the blue she dropped her bombshell. 'Neville and I are getting divorced,' she said.

'Y...?' Larch stared at her sister in astonishment, trying to take in what she thought she had just heard. 'You're...?'

'I've thrown Neville out!' Hazel announced.

'You've thrown...'

'Well, not physically, and it's going to cost me financially—he refused to go otherwise—but he's gone—went last night, and...' she paused '...you'll be pleased to learn he's not coming back.'

'*I'll* be pleased to learn?' Larch questioned faintly.

'You'll be delighted, or should be,' Hazel said. 'You don't have to pretend any more, love. And—neither do I.'

By then both of them were sitting down and had forgotten all about coffee, tea or breakfast. 'I thought you were— um—head over heels in love with him?' Larch gasped, coping with shock.

'I was one time, but that was so long ago I can barely remember.'

'But...'

Hazel smiled. 'Oh, I know I gave the impression that everything was all right in the Dawson camp. But with Mother so poorly, you looking after her, and Dad little short of demented at the thought of losing her, there was no way I was going to bring my troubles home.'

'Oh, Hazel, has it been so bad?'

'In a word—foul. Not to begin with,' she amended. 'At the beginning we were like two turtledoves. Then the philandering started. At first I couldn't believe it. I was all set to walk out then. But he asked forgiveness and said it would never happen again. I, like a fool, believed him.'

'It did happen again?' Larch asked, starting to get her breath back.

Hazel nodded. 'I don't suppose I heard of every occasion. But in the end it stopped hurting, and I realised I was out of love with him.'

Larch was still feeling staggered, but was trying to keep up with what Hazel was saying. 'But you didn't leave him?'

'He became something of a habit, and at the same time I started to get promoted higher and higher with Berry and Thacker. Besides, leaving him would have meant telling you and our parents, and I reckoned you'd all got enough on your collective plate to be going on with.'

'So you said nothing. You didn't even hint how bad things were.'

Hazel smiled wryly. 'They got worse. About the time Dad died, Neville's secretary came to the apartment and said she was pregnant. No need to guess who the father was. She had an abortion when Neville didn't want to know. But it was kind of the last straw. I knew then that I wanted to finish it. Then Mum died, and while you and I were dealing with our sadness and loss Neville revealed to me the giant hole his business was in.'

'You helped him out by selling the apartment.'

'To be honest, my first inclination was to let him sink. But he'd got a workforce dependent on him.'

'So you sold your lovely apartment and came home to live,' Larch supplied.

'Oh, love, I would never have done that had I known,' Hazel mourned, and looked so pained Larch knew she was truly hurting inside.

'Known?' she queried. 'Known what?'

Hazel gave a sorrowful shake of her head. 'What was I thinking of?' she muttered, clearly blaming herself. 'I knew Neville was not to be trusted with women, but it just didn't occur to me that he'd try out his "charms" on my baby sister.'

'You know about that!' Larch exclaimed, taken totally aback.

'I didn't—not until last night.'

'Does—does that have anything to do with why you're home? I thought you were staying in Denmark until the weekend.'

'I was. Until I rang Neville at his office yesterday. He's taken to sloping off in the evenings and at the weekend, so I rang to ask him to be around on Saturday, telling him that I wanted to have a serious talk with him.'

'He told you yesterday that he had—um—made a pass at me?' Larch asked hesitantly.

'To start with, no. To start with he seemed to guess what I wanted to talk to him about at the weekend. He went all bolshie, but said enough to make me certain that there was no way I was going to wait until the weekend to confront him. I went straight away to see Rune—Rune Pedersen, my head of department in Denmark,' she inserted with a hurried kind of breath. 'Rune arranged for me to catch the first available flight. I got in around the same time as Neville, and straight away told him I wanted a divorce.'

'I don't want you to break your marriage through anything connected with me!' Larch put in quickly.

'I'm not!' Hazel answered just as quickly, and, while Larch was wondering why Hazel suddenly appeared to be a little flushed, she went on to confess, 'Actually, I've—um—met someone else.'

'Hazel!' Larch gasped in astonishment.

'I know. Can you believe it? I never expected it, never thought I would ever fall in love again. But Rune...'

'It's Rune—your head of department in Denmark?'

'It is,' Hazel admitted. 'He's been so supportive. He's been through a divorce himself, so he's aware of the trauma you endure before you know without a single doubt that your marriage is over.'

'You know that now?' Larch asked gently.

'I fancy I've known it for a long while. Though at first, when Rune and I were initially attracted to each other, and I confessed what a sham my marriage was, I was still plagued with indecision about what I should do. I knew I should have phoned you more often, but I didn't want to risk having to speak to Neville. Nor did I want to come home at the weekends to spend time with him either, and blindly—I see that now—I thought you'd be okay during those weekends I was away in Denmark.'

This, Larch realised, explained why Hazel had appeared a little distracted when she had last seen her. 'You knew, when you went back to Denmark three weeks ago, that you'd be asking Neville for a divorce,' Larch probed gently.

'I imagine I did. I knew for certain anyway, when I got back and saw Rune again. I knew I didn't want to give up the sort of peace of mind I'd found with him. Though I have to say that peace of mind had been badly shattered prior to my going back when I learned about your accident. But when I'd rushed here and Tye said something about your consultant wanting you to have rest and quiet, I realised that, with hostilities between me and Neville about to turn into open warfare, it might be better if I kept you away from that rancorous atmosphere. Better for you if you stayed here until I'd got it all sorted. Tye seemed OK about it.'

'He's been extremely kind,' Larch replied quietly.

'It's a pity he's not here. Perhaps I'll have a chance to speak to him on the phone. I should have liked to thank him in person for the way he has so splendidly put himself out for you.'

'I—er...' Larch tried, dread starting to enter her heart as, shaken to the core, she realised what lay behind her sister's words.

'Shall I come and help you pack?' Hazel asked, confirming the worst.

'I'm—leaving here?' Larch questioned, her voice little more than a whisper even as she tried to hide just how completely devastated she suddenly felt.

'Oh, love, there's no need for you to worry,' Hazel said quickly, totally misinterpreting the reluctance to leave to be heard in Larch's voice. 'I told you, Neville is no longer back home. He moved out last night. I'll have to take out a mortgage on my share of the house to pay him off, but it will be worth it. When I think of him making a play for you, the...'

'He told you about it?'

'At first, no. When I rang from Denmark yesterday, to tell him I'd something to discuss this weekend, I also told him that I was hoping to have you back home by then.' This was news to Larch, but she realised that Hazel would have been thinking along the lines that once she had been pronounced fit by Miles Phipps on Friday there would no longer be any need for her to remain at Grove House. 'I told Neville that I didn't want you to be involved in any unpleasantness, and that I wanted our conversation to be away from the house. Anyhow, he must have suspected I intended to ask for a divorce, and he got nasty and determined he wasn't going to make it easy for me. He started by saying that you weren't the goody-goody I thought you were. That the real reason you were no longer working for him was because he'd sacked you after you'd gone to our bedroom one night and propositioned him.'

Larch was appalled. 'He said that!'

'Don't worry. I know him and you too well to believe that,' Hazel assured her. 'He's incapable of rejecting that sort of proposition. But I straight away began to fear that something had happened. Which, when I turned what he had said on its head, could mean only that *he* had come to your room one night and that *he* had propositioned you. I came home at once.'

'I'm sorry,' Larch apologised.

'Don't be.' Hazel smiled. 'I'd already made up my mind to end things between him and me, but had I not done so that would have clinched it. Up until then I was having pangs of guilt that I was in love with Rune and not my husband. But the moment Neville eventually admitted—and only then because he knew I would ask you if he didn't— that he'd angrily come to your room and—a polite word for it—attempted to seduce you, ice entered my heart. So—' she smiled suddenly '—ready to go?'

'I...' Larch hesitated. Even then, even when she knew that it was the answer—she would not even have to go and find herself a bedsit, but could go home—she hesitated.

'Don't you want to come home?' Hazel teased, seeing her hesitation. Then she realised what might be the reason for it. 'You think Tye will be offended when he comes back and finds you have left without saying a word?'

And that was when Larch bucked her ideas up. Only a short while ago Hazel had referred to how Tye had 'put himself out' for her. And Larch knew that he had, very much so. Were it not for her he would be residing in his London home and going about his normal social occupations.

'I'll write him a note,' Larch said with a smile, a knife twisting in her at the thought of him resuming his normal social occupations—a jealous knife. 'Jane will be here shortly. Can we wait until Jane gets here?'

'Of course we can.'

'You're not rushing back to Denmark?'

'No need,' Hazel replied, smiling. 'I've a few days' leave of absence. It was late by the time Neville left last night, too late for me to ring you, but Rune was waiting for my call. He's coming to England for the weekend.'

It took Larch an age to write her letter to Tye. She did

not want to leave, and felt she was bleeding inside. But with her sister now at home, and her brother-in-law not, from whichever way Larch looked at it she did not appear to have even the remotest excuse for staying. Eventually she wrote:

Dear Tye,
Hazel paid me an unexpected visit this morning—I thought she was still in Denmark. More unexpectedly, she called to say that she is divorcing Neville Dawson and that he has left our home. Which means I can now return there without cause for anxiety. Naturally I cannot leave without first thanking you so much for bringing me to Grove House and, with Jane, giving me such super care. I'm afraid I wasn't always an easy guest.

She still blushed when she thought of the way she had gone to his room that dreadful night and climbed into his bed—he must privately have been having forty fits.

But I honestly don't know what I would have done without you.
My warmest thanks, Larch.

She was not satisfied with what she had written, but knew that she could spend the whole morning in trying to compose something that showed him her gratitude but hid her love, and she still would not be satisfied. She went to his bedroom to leave her note, and felt tears close again when she glanced to the bed and flooding back came the memory of how she had awakened with Tye's arms around her. She recalled again those waking moments when she had felt safe and so secure. Everything had seemed so right then—everything so wrong now.

Jane, when she arrived, was surprised at the news that she was leaving, and gave her a warm hug. 'Thank you for…' Larch began.

'It was my pleasure.' Jane beamed, and came to wave them off.

Larch had always been the best of friends with her sister, but as she drove them home Larch was glad that Hazel had too much on her mind to want to talk very much.

With her thoughts mainly with Tye, Larch somehow got through the next twenty-four hours.

'Are you all right, Larch?' Hazel asked at one stage on Thursday. 'You're very quiet.'

'So are you,' Larch replied lightly.

'That's a point.' Hazel laughed. 'Does it show—that my thoughts are somewhere the other side of the North Sea?'

Larch smiled. 'Only a little,' she replied.

'You'll like him,' Hazel said. 'Rune,' she added, just in case there was any doubt about whom she was referring to. 'As it happens, you having your medical check-up in a London clinic will work out very well. We can go on from there to the airport to collect Rune tomorrow.'

'I—er—was thinking of cancelling my appointment,' Larch stated, wanting to see Miles, when he might mention Tye, while at the same time not wanting to hear him mention Tye's name in case he caught her at an unguarded moment and she somehow revealed her inner feelings. Larch owned she was feeling exceedingly vulnerable just then.

'No way!' her sister objected, but softened her words with a smile when she went on, 'When I think of how you nursed and cared for our mother, *and* kept the home going, then I think it's more than high time somebody looked after you.'

Somebody had looked after her, looked after her unbelievably well. Oh, Tye. 'But I'm fine now,' she said quickly. 'There's no need...'

'I don't think you fully realise just how traumatised you've been!' Hazel butted in firmly. 'Apart from your accident, you were still rocking from Mum and Dad, and that was before Neville came on to you. From what I've discovered, Miles Phipps has a first-class reputation. Keep your appointment. To please me, if nothing else?' she asked. 'I promise, once he says you're completely fit, we'll put everything behind us and we'll both start off afresh.'

Oh, that it was so simple. Larch wanted to look forward and not back, but it just wasn't that easy! How could she think of the future when Tye dominated almost her every thought? She did not want to dwell on the past, but time and again she remembered things he had said, things they had done together.

Just a simple walk with him had been magical. Driving through the countryside with Tye at the wheel so wonderful. 'You belong to me' he had told her once—oh, how she wished that were true and not said just from kindness because, back then, she'd had no one to belong to.

With a void in her heart, an ache for Tye, regret in her every step that she had ever left Grove House, Friday at last dragged its way into being. Larch knew that to leave Grove House had been her only option, for goodness' sake. Pride demanded that she did not become a burden to Tye and outstay her welcome, but pride did not make her feel any the less heartsore.

He would return home that morning, and she felt guilty that, but for her, he would probably have stayed where he was, working somewhere.

After an early lunch, Hazel appeared anxious to be on their way to the clinic. In love herself, Larch fully appreciated that her sister was probably counting the minutes until she saw Rune again. But, having started out early, they were way too early at the clinic for Larch's appointment.

With neither of them wanting to bother with refreshments, they waited in the car until nearer her appointment time, which gave Larch an opportunity to discuss something she had been mulling over in an attempt to stop thinking of Tye every other minute.

'I've been thinking, Hazel,' she began.

'Dangerous territory,' Hazel quipped, plainly feeling on top of the world.

'The thing is, I can't imagine that you'll want to stay permanently living at home if Rune is living in Denmark.'

Hazel was silent for a second or two, but, looking over to her, confessed, 'I was going to save this conversation until after you'd seen Miles Phipps today, but since you've brought it up—I've decided to apply for a transfer to Denmark. That doesn't—'

'It's the obvious thing to do,' Larch butted in. 'What I've thought,' she went on, 'is that since I shan't want to live in that big house on my own, we could sell it and—'

'Are you serious?' Hazel interrupted in surprise.

Larch nodded. 'I'm not sure what training I want to do yet, but if the college I choose is out of the area, then I could buy a small flat with my half, and—'

'You're not suggesting this purely so I won't have to go into debt to pay Neville off?' Hazel took her turn, in the way sisters have, to butt in.

That too had figured in Larch's thoughts. It seemed criminal to her that when Neville had been such an awful husband Hazel was going to have to go into debt for a huge mortgage before she could find happiness in her new beginnings.

'It just isn't logical for me to stay in that big house on my own,' Larch answered. 'I wouldn't want to.'

'You could come to Denmark and live with Rune and me,' Hazel suggested at once.

'I'll come and see you as often as I can,' Larch replied, and would not be persuaded to make her proposed visits any more permanent than that.

What she wanted—really, really wanted—was to live where Tye lived, be it Grove House or his London address. She sighed hopelessly, then, when she saw Hazel glance swiftly to her, she beamed a smile.

'Let's go and see if Miles is running early,' she suggested.

They found that in actual fact he was running late. 'I'm terribly sorry, Mr Phipps had to deal with an urgent emergency. He's running about three quarters of an hour behind time,' the woman on the desk apologised.

Larch was all for cancelling her appointment, but Hazel would not hear of it. 'We'll wait,' she said firmly.

'But it might make you late getting to the airport!' Larch reminded her.

Hazel did look a shade pulled two ways, but insisted, 'We'll wait.'

The three quarters of an hour delay proved to be out by fifteen minutes, and it had gone four by the time a nurse came and took Larch in to see Miles Phipps. 'Larch,' he greeted her pleasantly. 'You're looking so much better. Come and tell me how you've been.'

For all he was by then running well over an hour late, he appeared in no hurry whatsoever. And it was a full half an hour later that he completed every one of his very detailed tests. Then he shook her by the hand.

'You've made a splendid recovery,' he pronounced. And he smiled a lovely warm smile as he charmingly added, 'Regrettably, it will not be necessary for me to see you again.'

Larch smiled back. He had not mentioned Tye, this man who was her last link with the man she loved. She did not mention Tye either. 'Goodbye,' she said, and thanked Miles, and went from his office knowing that, having just been discharged as his patient, having been declared fit, she should be in high spirits—when in actual fact her spirits were somewhere down on the floor.

She wanted Tye. She wanted him to be there. She wanted to be able to tell him that his stepbrother had just deleted her name from his clinic list. That, fit once more, her case papers would now be filed permanently away.

Oh, Tye. She loved him so, and by now he had probably read her note, and was no doubt very much relieved that, by leaving, she had saved him the chore of driving her to Roselands clinic today.

She swallowed hard, then raised her head a fraction before turning the corner and going into the waiting room where, some thirty minutes or so ago, she had left Hazel.

There were several people in the various chairs in the waiting room. But Hazel was not amongst them. Realising that, with time going on, Hazel was most likely in the car park with the car engine running, Larch picked up speed and went hurrying towards the outer swing doors.

But only to almost cannon in to a tall, dark-haired man who was about to come in. 'S...' she began to apologise. But as she looked up, so her apology never made it. 'T-Tye!' she stammered, scarlet colour flooding her face, her heart at once thundering.

'Hello, Larch,' he replied calmly, and, placing a hand on her arm, he helped her free of the door and to the outside. And there, as nice as you please, he bent and placed a light kiss on her cheek, and, looking down at her, stood back to ask, 'What have you got to tell me?'

CHAPTER NINE

'WHAT are you doing here?' Larch gasped, and, still flushed from the emotion of seeing him again, not to mention his unexpected kiss, felt herself going red again as the answer to that question came rushing at her. 'Of course—you've come to see Miles. He's running late. He...' She stopped. She was gabbling—and Tye still had a hold of her arm. 'I left you a note,' she said, and felt hot all over at the inadequacy of that remark. 'Hazel's in the car park,' she added, and determined that henceforth she would shut up.

But, 'She isn't,' Tye replied evenly.

'She isn't?'

'We said hello. I was able to explain, that running late or not, Miles would still insist on giving you a very detailed final check. Your sister seemed a little anxious to be at the airport,' Tye informed her blandly. 'Apparently she has a date with a very special Dane.' Larch stared at him wordlessly—Hazel had confided in him about Rune Pedersen? But Larch's surprises were not yet over when Tye followed up with, 'Hazel knew she could trust me when I suggested if she wanted to go that I would give you a lift home.'

Larch's mouth fell open. 'Oh, I couldn't let you!' she exclaimed quickly.

'Why couldn't you?'

She was momentarily stumped. 'Because...well, you've already done so much for me. And—and Warren End is miles out of your way.' Larch got herself more together. 'I can get a train and—'

'And put me in your sister's bad books for ever?' he cut in.

Larch looked at him, and loved him, and because she

168

loved him and had missed him so much she could not hold
out any longer. She gave in, and went with him to the car
park. She knew she was being greedy, but she could not
resist this unthought chance to spend a little more time with
the man who held her heart. Involuntarily her hand went to
the cheek he had kissed, and she was entranced for a moment. That kiss of greeting had seemed almost as if, pleased
to see her, he could not hold back on the impulse.

Rats, said her saner self, and as they reached his car and
he opened the passenger door for her she knew she was
going to have to guard against such weird thoughts. 'Er—
Hazel would have waited,' Larch felt a need to say when
Tye came round and got in beside her.

'Without question she would,' he agreed, and paused for
a second or two, then added evenly, 'As a matter of fact,
though, I rather wanted to have a word or two with you.'

Larch turned to look at him. 'What about?' she asked,
but he was busy switching on the ignition and did not appear
to have heard. And, since he seemed to be concentrating on
getting his long sleek car out of the overcrowded car park
without mishap, she did not repeat her question.

The traffic was heavy, and rather than distract him in any
small way she stayed silent while he negotiated the route.
She was unfamiliar with London streets, but when some ten
minutes later she began anticipating that Tye would shortly
be making for the motorway, she was a little surprised when
he drove into the forecourt of a very imposing-looking
apartment block.

She looked questioningly at him. 'I need to stop and pick
something up,' he said by way of explanation.

'You—is this where you live?'

'Come up,' he invited. 'I shouldn't be too long, but then
again...' He left the words in the air and, having been prepared to wait for him in the car, she picked up a hint there
that he might be delayed—perhaps taking an unexpected
phone call or something—and could do no other than give

in to the sudden urge to see inside his apartment. She could not expect to see him after today, she knew, but it would be a bonus to be able to imagine him inside his apartment. Perhaps relaxing, unwinding after a busy day. Maybe reading his newspaper…

'All right,' she agreed, and went with him into the smart building, and into the lift with him up to the top floor.

He showed her into his high-ceilinged, elegant, uncluttered drawing room. There were a couple of oil paintings on one wall, a couple of sofas, a couple of well-padded chairs, low tables—she was glad she had seen the room.

'Have a seat,' Tye invited, seeming in no hurry at all to collect what he had come for. Larch went to the nearest seat, a sofa, and for no reason all at once felt a degree nervous. She did not know why. She would trust Tye with her life. Perhaps it was that small sense of tension that was in the air. 'Would you like some tea?' he asked nicely, proof if she needed it that he had no immediate hurry.

Larch relaxed a little, and even smiled at Tye, realising that he must be aware that, for all there was a small restaurant at the clinic, that she had been hanging around for ages that afternoon without refreshment.

'Let me make it,' she volunteered, grateful for any chance to spend a few more minutes with him. 'You've been working and—'

'I took the day off,' Tye interrupted.

'Oh!' That took her a little aback. 'You've—um—been busy, though, I expect.'

'You could say that,' he replied, and to her surprise, instead of heading to either the kitchen or to go and collect what they were there for, he came and took a chair close by. 'I worked until the early hours this morning,' he said.

'Oh,' she murmured again, and as her brain slowly woke up she began to associate the word 'work' with something else he had said. 'You said you wanted to have a word or two with me,' she remembered, and her heart suddenly started to race—was he going to offer her a job after all? Oh, for the chance to see him occasionally when he was at his office…

'That's true,' he agreed, but paused for long moments, strangely as though choosing his words very carefully. Then he said, 'I was surprised to read your note on Wednesday.'

She hadn't expected that, and pushed her shining blonde hair back from her face in a nervous kind of gesture. 'You read…' Her voice dried. 'On Wednesday? You went back to Grove House on Wednesday?' Her lovely blue eyes widened. 'I didn't think you were going back there until today?'

'That was my original intention,' he accepted, his grey eyes steady on her, watching, taking in, reading. Swiftly she lowered her eyes. But hurriedly raised them to stare in disbelief when he continued, 'But when nobody seemed to be around when several times I rang Grove House, I thought I had better contact Jane Harris.'

'Oh, Tye. Jane told you I'd gone with Hazel. But…' Larch hesitated. 'You didn't leave your work because of me? Of course you didn't,' she contradicted, at once feeling foolish.

Though she felt more speechless than foolish when he confirmed, 'I did.' She stared wordlessly at him, and he went on, 'I couldn't believe you had gone—just like that.'

'You—read the note I left, you said.'

Tye gave an impatient movement, and then half terrified her by saying shortly, 'I thought there was more between us than some polite little letter.'

He knows! He knows I'm in love with him! Larch looked swiftly away from him, realising that the tension she had felt earlier came solely from her, and her fear that he might see the love she had for him.

'You didn't get to see M-Miles today?' she said, rapidly changing the subject, ready then to latch on to anything other than her and Tye and what was between them. Without a doubt he was referring to the way she had clung on to him on Tuesday night.

'I didn't need to see Miles.'

'Oh,' she murmured, unsure what to make of that. Surely, had Miles not been running so late with his outpatients clinic, Tye would have waited around to discuss whatever it was he had gone to the clinic to see him about. 'You'll be glad to know I was discharged as perfectly fit today,' she offered brightly.

'I know,' Tye replied. And that caused her to look at him again.

'You know?' she questioned. And, her brain on the meddle again, 'How do you know? Even Hazel doesn't know y—'

'At the risk of Miles being thought unethical—though I have to say there is a great deal he and I would do for each other—Miles rang my mobile, where I was stationed at Roselands entrance, the second you left his office.'

Larch stared at Tye open-mouthed. 'You...' She tried again. 'You arranged with him that he should ring you...'

'You obviously didn't want me to come with you today.'

'Oh, Tye. It wasn't like that!' she protested. Had she, by leaving the way she had, hurt his feelings? Surely not! But her brain, that always had sought to know more, was on the search again. 'You weren't there to—at the clinic—to see Miles?' she asked slowly. 'But...' her heartbeats were suddenly thundering '...but to see me?'

He did not deny it. 'I knew you'd be there.'

He had been there purposely to see her! Her hand went nervously to her hair again. 'How?' she asked, a dozen and one things starting to chase around in her head. 'How did you know I'd be there? I didn't want to go,' she admitted. 'I was all for cancelling my appointment with Miles.'

'Your sister would never allow you to miss your appointment,' Tye remarked confidently.

Larch looked at him sitting there, leaning slightly forward, his eyes on nowhere but her. How dear he was to her. But this would never do! Somehow she found a cheery note. 'Well, I'd better start making tracks for Warren End!' she said. She would have got to her feet then, only so smoothly, and without apparent haste, before she could do more than collect her bag from the side of her, Tye had left his chair and was all at once sitting next to her.

Then, while she was feeling pink, red, all colours, he had taken a hold of her right hand and was preventing her from going anywhere. 'We haven't had our—discussion yet,' he said calmly.

She wished she could feel as calm. 'D-discussion?' she stammered. And, managing to get herself a little under control, 'This is the word or two you wanted to have with me?'

'I never intended our talk to be all one-way,' he replied, his tone a tinge warmer, she rather thought, though she would not be surprised if she had that wrong. With Tye sitting so near, it seemed to be closing down her thinking capability.

'W-what's the subject?' she queried, somehow thinking it would be better if she hadn't asked, but her curiosity choosing that moment to want to have its twopenny worth.

Tye looked at her, his grip on her hand firming—every bit as if he was the one feeling tense and not her. 'Us,' he very clearly said.

Had she been free there was every chance she would have bolted. But her right hand was held firmly in his grip and it did not look as if he was going to allow her to bolt anywhere in a hurry. 'Us?' she echoed faintly. And, because he was good and kind, and because she had no option, 'Oh, Tye, there is no us,' she said. She thought he went a little pale, but she wasn't taking heed of her imagination just then. Tye had been so wonderful to her, but she was nothing to him. 'I know I was a bit clingy on Tuesday night.' She went red, 'Well, a lot clingy, actually, when we—you know. But you don't have to be kind to me and—'

'Who the hell's being kind?' he cut in, startling her by his sudden aggressiveness.

'You've seen—' She broke off with a catch of breath. Oh, my stars, she had so nearly told him that she loved him!

'I've seen quite a lot.' He took over when she abruptly ran out of words. 'I've seen you ill, scared, brave, proud. I've seen *you* kind, and I have wanted to do all I could for you...'

'Tye, you did!' she exclaimed urgently. 'I've put you to so much trouble.'

'No, you haven't,' he denied.

But she was not having that. 'When I think of how I got into your bed that night—' she began for starters, but was again interrupted by him.

'Something you would never dream of doing had I not given you the impression that we lived together and that you were no stranger to my bed,' Tye cut in, his aggression suddenly gone.

Larch looked at him, glad he wasn't angry with her any more; she did not want him angry with her. 'Can we be friends?' she asked.

'I'd like that,' he answered, and, while that pleased her, she thought she had better go now. But when she again went to gather up her bag prior to leaving, 'Not yet,' Tye said quietly.

'I don't want—' she began, above all not wanting him to know that she was hopelessly in love with him.

But he was again cutting in. 'And what about what I want?' he asked quietly.

And Larch dropped her bag and turned and looked into his steady grey eyes. Were it in her power she would give him anything in the world he wanted. 'What is it you want?' she asked—and was stunned by his reply.

Though first he took a long drawn breath, and then, his other hand coming to take a hold of her left hand, he looked deeply into her eyes. 'You,' he said. 'I want you, Larch.'

Wordlessly, barely breathing, she stared at him. Her brain seemed to have seized up. 'You don't,' she denied huskily.

'I do.' His look was unflinching.

'But, but…' She took a steadying breath. 'But on Tuesday, when we…' She faltered again. 'You could have… You know I would have—um—made love with you. Only you didn't want to.'

His amazement was obvious. 'Are you mad?' he asked incredulously. 'Didn't want to! Ye gods, I was desperate for you!'

'Desperate? You—were?'

'You *must* have known I—' He broke off. 'Oh, my dear,' he said softly, 'You had no idea in your innocence of what it took me to break away from you that night.'

She stared at him, feeling slightly stunned. 'I th-thought I'd been too clinging,' she said faintly.

'Clinging? You?'

'Paulette said something about—'

'Oh, Larch,' Tye cut in. 'Much as I am very fond of my stepsister-in-law, would you now, and in the future, take most of what she babbles on about with the proverbial grain of salt?'

Now *and* in the future! Larch was starting to grow confused, so decided to concentrate solely on what Tye was saying—subject: us. 'But…' She was about to argue, then changed it to, 'I wasn't clinging? I thought I was. You said you should let me go, only I wouldn't let you.'

'I haven't forgotten. In fact—' his look was deadly serious '—in fact,' he continued, 'thinking about the way you were with me had me awake most of that night.'

'Because—you wanted to make love with me?' she asked, feeling not a little fog-bound.

'That, of course,' he agreed. 'But more particularly I spent many wakeful night hours wanting to believe, yet being afraid to believe, that you were perhaps just a little…'

he paused '…in love with me…' His grip on her hands was firm when she would have jerked out of his hold.

'Well, of course I'm fond of you,' she said hurriedly, borrowing his word for his feelings for his stepsister-in-law in a panicky rush of defence. 'Who wouldn't have grown fond of you in the circumstances?'

She thought that he again briefly lost some of his colour, but she was inwardly panicking too wildly to know anything for sure but that she should never have been so weak as to have got into his car. Greed, that was what it had been. She had greedily given in to her need to spend more time with him.

But Tye was shaking his head. 'No,' he said.

'No?' she echoed, her throat more than a touch dry.

'It has to be more than that.'

Fondness, did he mean? 'I'm sorry,' she apologised, hoping he would think she was sorry she could not be a little in love with him.

His eyes were fixed on her as he studied her, and she began to feel nervous again. It was as though he was trying to see into her very soul. And she could not have that. Though when she would have said something, said anything to break the silence, Tye shook his head. 'No,' he said again. 'I have spent more time than you can know over these last few days dissecting every word, every look, every nuance that has passed between us.' He gave her hands a small shake. 'I can't believe—'

'I don't want this conversation!' Larch cut in bluntly, inwardly drowning in panic.

But his study of her was unrelenting. Then all at once a hint of a smile tugged at the corners of his mouth. 'I'm scaring you?' he asked, every bit as though he had just discerned exactly what she was scared about—his guessing at so much as the tiniest bit of love she had for him.

'I think I'll go home now,' she stated shortly. Only found,

when his hands came to her arms, that she was going nowhere until he was ready.

'Don't be alarmed. There's nothing to be afraid of,' Tye promised her soothingly.

She wished she could believe that, but since she could not get away without some undignified push and shove, she did the only thing possible. 'I'm not interested in your lies!' She went into the attack.

'Lies!' He seemed surprised.

'You wanted to make love to me but, as desperate as you were, you calmly walked away that night.'

'*Calmly!* My recollection of it is that I bolted while I still could.'

'A likely tale!' she jibed, though clearly recalled that he had left his shirt behind, he had been in such a hurry to go.

That hint of a smile was coming to the corners of his mouth again, every bit as if he had just seen through her attack and had recognised it for what it was—an attempt to put him off. 'You're not going to make this easy for me, are you, sweetheart?' he questioned gently.

She almost softened on the spot at his tone, never mind the bone-melting 'sweetheart'. 'You're blaming all this on me—and I hardly know what all this *is*,' she burst out chokily. 'Other than it's all to do with you wanting me, but denying your need. I...'

'How could I do anything other?' he asked.

And that made her cross. 'There you are, confusing me again!' she exclaimed. 'I'd rather have answers than questions—if you don't mind.'

'You shall have anything it's in my power to give you,' Tye replied, and she wished her imagination would behave, because she distinctly thought she saw a certain kind of tenderness in his eyes.

'That sounds promising!' How she managed to answer so snappily, when what she wanted to do was to throw herself at him and ask him to hold her, she did not know. But what he said next almost had her in a state of total collapse.

For he smiled, and then he tenderly, definitely tenderly, said, 'Forgive me if I'm going about this all the wrong way, but you have wound your way into my heart, Larch Burton, and it has rather messed up my previous, prior to knowing you, totally logical way of thinking.'

Absolutely thunderstruck, she stared at him. 'Er—well, maybe I will st-stay a little bit longer,' she conceded with what voice she could find. And was glad she was sitting down when he leaned forward and placed a light kiss on the corner of her mouth.

That was when her voice went completely, and, feeling all of a tremble, all she was capable of was just to sit there and stare at him. Had he *really* said that she had wound her way into his heart?

'You really are the most beautiful delight to me,' Tye said softly, and kissed the other corner of her mouth before pulling back. 'You're distracting me again,' he charged, then seemed to get himself more together, muttering, 'Logical order,' and, while she was still looking a touch staggered at him, he began, 'So there was I, at the hospital to see Miles, when you were wheeled in.'

'This is going back to...'

'To when I first saw you, beautiful, broken and bloodied, but not as broken as I at first thought. Poor love, you did look in a state. Then, when I promise you I seldom do anything without considered thought, I find that under the pretext of going to the hospital to see Miles I'm going to the hospital to check on your progress.'

'You came more than once.'

'I became a regular visitor. As we both know, your only visitor.'

'You still came to visit me—even when I came out of the coma,' Larch said, her heart racing, seeming to stop, start, and race on again.

Tye grinned self-deprecatingly. 'I naturally told myself I
was only going to see you so I should get my grandmother's
ring back.' His grin faded. 'Then we realised you had lost
your memory, and such a feeling of wanting to keep you
safe came over me that, when you asked, ''Am I engaged
to you?'', looking so lost and alone—you had no one—I
just wanted you to have someone. There was simply no way
I could tell you no. There was no way either,' he added,
'that, while I admit I didn't quite trust what was happening
to me, I was going to let you leave the clinic to adjust to a
life with no memory with anyone but me.'

'Oh, Tye,' she whispered. He didn't trust what was happening to him? What? What was it that he did not trust?
She was impatient suddenly to learn. But so far her confusion had cleared, and she did not want it to return, so
thought perhaps she had better let things go at the pace he
set.

'When Miles agreed I might take you to the peace and
quiet of Grove House, I said I would keep in close touch
with him.'

'You rang him…?'

'Constantly,' Tye replied. 'I almost got him out of bed
that night when things were at their very darkest for you
and you came flying into my room. While it was continually
in my head that for all I knew you might be married or be
in some serious relationship, I had to quickly decide whether
to try and calm you myself or ring Miles and wait for him
to arrive. Your need seemed more urgent than to wait. I
gave in to my need to cradle you better. I thought I had
made the right decision when at last you started to relax and
finally fell asleep.'

'And when I woke up my memory was back,' she
supplied.

'Your memory had returned, and before I knew it you
were talking of how you'd disrupted my household, disrupted my work,' he reminded her, but was gripping her

firmly when he added, 'And I didn't feel it appropriate at that time to mention just how much you had disrupted—me.'

Larch blinked, her eyes widening. 'Er...' was as far as she could manage. 'Um—how do you mean?' She got a little farther.

'For one,' he began without hesitation, 'you seemed to be forever talking of leaving.'

'Forever?' she challenged mildly.

'I was sensitive on the subject,' he said with a grin. 'You said you had no hold on me, but, my dear, you had.' And, while her heart started to furiously race again, 'A hold on my heart,' he said softly.

'Oh, Tye,' Larch whispered shakily, and didn't feel any less shaky when he placed a tender kiss on her lovely mouth.

'What's a man to do?' he asked. 'You're there in my head the whole time, yet you're talking of leaving.'

'You found me a job putting those books on the computer,' she reminded him, having to latch on to something factual while she coped with the fact that Tye had said she had a hold on his heart.

'Which you at first declined.'

'Until you blackmailed me into staying.'

'I certainly wasn't going to allow you to return to your brother-in-law's orbit,' Tye said forthrightly. But he was gentle when he asked, 'You have me where you want me, Larch Burton, so what are you going to do about it?'

She smiled; she loved him so. And he had actually said she had a hold on his heart. She had heard him say it. 'I'm not terribly sure,' she answered, and loved him enough to dare to confess, 'I have—er—grown to be quite—er—um—care for you.'

'Care?' he took up, his eyes on hers. 'Care as in, it's burning a hole in your gut? That kind of caring?'

Her lips parted in surprise. 'You—know the feeling?'

'It's a feeling I live with,' he answered, and added those two magical words, 'for you.'

'Oh, Tye,' she murmured tremulously, and was drawn suddenly into the circle of his arm.

Her heart was beating so she could hardly breathe. And when Tye looked deeply into her lovely blue eyes and said, 'I love you, my darling,' she felt on the point of collapse. He loved her! He loved her. Had he actually said those three wonderful words? He bent and kissed her. She did not resist and, perhaps heartened that she did not, Tye pulled back and asked, 'Can you tell me now if it's possible you love me a little?'

'You know,' she answered shyly.

He shook his head. 'Trust me. I need to hear it. Need to hear you say it.'

She looked at him, her heart in her eyes. 'Little is such a puny word.' Shyly, she added, 'Tye, I love you with all of my heart.'

Larch was not conscious of time passing when in the next five minutes he held her close, kissed her, still holding her close. Then it seemed he just had to look into her face. Look into her face and kiss and hold her again. And Larch, such joy in her heart that Tye loved her in return, held him and returned his kisses, marvelling at his love for her, and that she no longer had to hide her love for him.

But it was Tye, finally leaning back to let daylight between them, who commented, 'I can hardly believe this. I've been half off my head about you, and here you are...'

'Have you? Been half off your head?' she whispered, totally enthralled.

'You have no idea.'

Her smile beamed. Was this really, really happening? 'When...? Why...?'

'When did I start loving you? Why? Where do I start?' He paused to kiss her and to cradle her lovingly against him. 'It began with my heart giving a leap the very first time I laid eyes on you. It could be—and was, I assured myself—totally because I was unused to seeing road traffic accident victims at such close quarters. Then, when I continued to come to the hospital to personally check on your progress, there started to grow in me such a fierce feeling of wanting to protect you. And from there I found I wanted to be with you, to talk to you—to be your companion, if you like. Then one day at Grove House you asked, "Do I belong to someone?". And while I fully appreciated just how very dreadful it must be for you to have absolutely no memory of family or friends, I knew right then that it did not matter who you were. You were mine and I was in love with you.'

Larch clearly remembered it. It was shortly after he had taken her to Grove House. 'You've loved me since then?' she asked in wonderment.

'I've been enchanted by you,' he confessed. 'I nearly told you as much that Sunday we took a walk around the village. I just couldn't stop myself from kissing you. And for my sins made myself scarce the next week, while I tried to get myself under control. By then, sweet love, I found that my love for you included a need to hold you in my arms, to kiss and embrace you. Which meant that the only way I could cope was to not let you get close. I came home at the end of that week...'

'It was a Friday, two weeks ago,' Larch recalled without effort. 'You were a pig,' she said lovingly.

'Oh, I was,' he thoroughly agreed. 'Until I saw I had upset you. I came after you and held you in my arms—and wanted to hold you like that for evermore.'

'Why couldn't you?'

'You loved me then?'

'I loved you then,' Larch answered.

'When? Since when?' he demanded.

'Since that day I got my memory back,' she answered instantly. 'We were having dinner that night, you and me, and—I just knew I was in love with you. It was just there, and whether I wanted it or not it was not going to go away.'

'Oh, my darling,' he murmured, and held her close up against him while he lingeringly kissed her. Her heart was pounding anew when Tye pulled back. 'That's why,' he said.

'That's why what?' she asked, completely mesmerised by the warmth of feeling, that hint of passion in his kiss.

'You asked why couldn't I hold you for ever,' he reminded her. 'That's why. You still had two weeks to go before you saw Miles—I was beginning to feel the strain.'

'Oh, love,' she whispered.

'It was only a week later that I was kissing you again, while at the same time assuring you that I would never take advantage of your innocence.'

'You are a spoilsport,' she teased, and loved it that she could.

'Talk like that is going to get you into very serious trouble,' he threatened with a humorous growl, but went on, 'It was around then that my normal logical thinking processes started to become clouded.'

'*Clouded?*' she repeated. Tye struck her as a man whose thought processes never got fogged up. 'I know I've been up to my neck in confusion, but—you?'

'With what logic I could find, I had to make a decision,' he answered. 'I knew I loved you, and that I wanted you, but I had to decide not to do anything about it until Miles said you were completely recovered, completely well.'

'You wanted to hear that I was fully well before...'

'Before I could set about asking you out—not as my house guest but as my woman-friend. My intention had been to come with you today to see Miles, and as soon as he gave you a clean bill of health we'd go out for that celebratory dinner and I would begin my courting campaign.'

'Oh, Tye!' Larch sighed. 'And I ruined it for you by leaving Grove House!'

'And left me wondering if my plan to give you "personal" attention was ever going to get off the ground. What if you did not want my personal attention? It looked very much as if you didn't. And yet I just couldn't let you disappear out of my life.'

Larch stared at him open-mouthed. By the sound of it Tye had been in the same stewed-up world that she had. 'But you knew on Tuesday night, when, despite what you say, I did cling on to you, that I was—er—receptive.'

'Oh, my darling,' he breathed. 'When I left your room that night...'

'Why did you?' she asked, going a pretty shade of pink and adoring him when, seeing her colour, he smiled a tender smile. 'I mean, if *you* didn't think I was clinging...'

'I had to leave you, my love,' Tye said gently. 'I'd not many days before assured you I would never take advantage of you, yet there you were, inexperienced, in my arms—and still had a medical check to go through. Your health seemed fine to me—but what did I know? I wasn't trained to spot any small—'

'Oh, my poor love,' she interrupted softly. 'All that went through your head while you were telling me you had better go?'

He nodded. 'It was a torturous night,' he owned. 'But as I went through everything that was between us, every wonderful facet I knew of you, I suddenly began to hope. And all at once I was torn between wanting to believe, and being afraid to believe, what all my instincts were telling me.'

'That I might love you a little?'

His arms tightened around her. 'I tried to scoff at the notion, but again and again I seemed to come to the same conclusion. You didn't hate me; that was fairly certain.'

'You asked if I hated you when you came to my room on Wednesday morning,' she reminded him with a loving smile.

'I was unsure of my reception,' he said with a grin. 'Part

of me wanted to tell you straight away how it was with me, while at the same time I was afraid of rushing you. I wanted to ask you to throw some clothes on and come with me—while common sense tripped me up. I'd be involved with business for the next couple of days—what fun would that be for you? So it was back to my original plan.'

'Your plan to…'

'My plan to wait until Miles said you were completely well, and so gave me permission to come courting you.'

'Oh, Tye.' She could hardly believe any of this. It was all so marvellous. To her delight, Tye bent and kissed her in a way that was so filled with love she was speechless when he drew back.

He smiled into her eyes, but it took him several seconds before he remembered. 'Hmm—that was a couple of days ago. But I was impatient. Friday seemed an impossibly long way away. I tried to ring you—and discovered my wait was going to be even more stressful than I had imagined.'

'You went home—to Grove House.'

'I couldn't believe you'd gone!'

'I'm sorry.' She loved him so much she could not bear to think how her leaving the way she had must have hurt him. 'I love you,' she whispered, and reached up and kissed him.

More heart-stoppingly wonderful seconds passed as they kissed and held each other, then Tye was drawing back from her so he could see into her face. 'You said in your letter that you honestly didn't know what you would have done without me.' Larch looked into his grey eyes, her heart racing at the love and warmth in them for her.

'I meant every word,' she replied huskily.

'May I tell you then, my dear, my very dear, adorable Larch, that I am so deeply in love with you that I honestly don't know what *I* will do, without you in my life?'

'Tye.' She breathed his name.

He tenderly kissed her, then let go of her with one arm

while he found something in his pocket. 'Remember this?' he asked, and showed her his grandmother's ring.

It was a lovely memory. 'You haven't given it to Paulette yet?'

'I no longer intend to.'

'You—don't?' Larch queried.

He caught hold of her left hand. 'Until I can get you a ring of your choosing, would you wear this one?' he asked.

'What are you s-saying?' she asked tremulously, her insides all of a tremble once more.

Tye looked sincerely into her wide blue eyes. 'I'm saying, my darling, that I love you with all of my heart. That I cannot think of a life without you. And that I would like it very much if you would marry me.'

'You want to marry me?' she gasped. 'But—but—you once agreed it was highly unlikely that you would ever marry! You said so.'

'It would appear I'm better at putting up a smokescreen than I thought,' he answered with a smile. 'I knew then, as I said it, that I was having dinner with the woman I was hoping would be my wife.'

She was staring at him in amazement, tears very near. 'Oh, Tye,' she cried softly.

'Is that a yes or a no?' he asked, and only then did she notice the sudden look of strain on his face as he waited for her answer.

She smiled lovingly at him. 'We both know the ring fits,' she whispered.

And Tye slid the ring home on her engagement finger. 'I'm taking that as a yes,' he said. She was too full to speak, so nodded, and with a joyous smile breaking on his face, 'Come here,' he said, his voice gruff with emotion. But it was tenderly that he held her and kissed her—his fiancée.

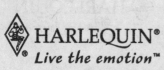

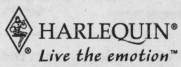

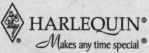

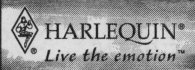